A Dusk of Demons

John Christopher

PUFFIN BOOKS

PUFFIN BOOKS

Published by the Penguin Group
Penguin Books Ltd, 27 Wrights Lane, London W8 5TZ, England
Penguin Books USA Inc., 375 Hudson Street, New York, New York 10014, USA
Penguin Books Australia Ltd, Ringwood, Victoria, Australia
Penguin Books Canada Ltd, 10 Alcorn Avenue, Toronto, Ontario, Canada M4V 3B2
Penguin Books (NZ) Ltd, 182–190 Wairau Road, Auckland 10, New Zealand

Penguin Books Ltd, Registered Offices: Harmondsworth, Middlesex, England

First published by Hamish Hamilton Ltd 1993
Published in Puffin Books 1994
1 3 5 7 9 10 8 6 4 2

Text copyright © John Christopher, 1993
All rights reserved

The moral right of the author has been asserted

Printed in England by Clays Ltd, St Ives plc

PUFFIN BOOKS

A Dusk of Demons

John Christopher was born in Lancashire in 1922, but moved to Hampshire when he was ten. After demobilization from the army in 1946 he tried his hand at writing. His main ambition was aimed at the mainstream of fiction, but in the interests of supporting a growing family he ventured into other fields, writing thrillers, cricket novels, light comedy and also the science fiction to which he had been addicted in his early teens. Since 1958 he has been a full-time writer. In the late sixties he was asked to write for young people: the resulting Tripods trilogy prefigured two other trilogies and a total of sixteen works of speculative fiction. He is married, with children and grandchildren, and lives in Rye, East Sussex.

In memoriam:
Charlotte Louise de Putron
aged twenty
a brave destroyer of Demons

I

I awoke with the early morning sun dazzling my eyes. This was not in itself unusual because my window faced east, but it triggered a sense of something being wrong. There had been a bothering light in my eyes the night before, from the full moon, and in the end I had climbed out of bed and drawn the curtains against its brilliance. Yet they were open now.

That was when I remembered the nightmare. I'd had nightmares before, when I was little – I could call up hazy recollections of smoke and fire and fear – but there had been nothing like that for years. I had slept, in those days, in a cot beside Mother Ryan's bed, and been lifted in beside her to be comforted. Last night too, Mother Ryan had provided comfort, but she must have come the length of the corridor to reach me. She had sat on the edge of my bed, trying to persuade me there was nothing to be frightened of. In the end, she had left me and gone to the window, and opened the curtains to show me there really was nothing out there but moonlight. Even then I had taken some convincing.

It had seemed so real! And yet it was a reality without shape. I had known there were things outside, but could not tell what sort of things they were. All I was conscious of was that howling, ebbing and swelling as they circled the house. Each time it died down I thought they might be going away, but each time they came back and there seemed to be more of them than before.

My one concern was to escape – hide under the bed, or better still run and find somewhere in the house where I could not hear them. But I could not even sit up: my legs refused to move and a dead weight pinned my shoulders. Then the shapeless voices stopped circling and were wailing monstrously against my window. Glass could not hold against such a volume of sound . . . and as I thought that, it shattered, and I knew they were in the room with me.

I suppose that was when I started yelling, still not knowing what they were and not daring to look. It seemed a long time before Mother Ryan was beside me, telling me to hush, it was only a bad dream – urging me to open my eyes and see there was no one there but her – no sounds except those of the distant sea and the wind in the pines, and her voice, part chiding but more reassuring.

'It's Andy's the cause of it, the little-good-for. He was at the Master's brandy again yesterday, and when the liquor's in him his tongue flaps nonsense. But I'm astonished at you paying heed to him. You should be used to his blather.'

Had I been thinking clearly, it would have surprised me too. I'd known he was drunk when he came in, from his careful, stiff way of walking. I hadn't believed a word of his ramblings about the black Demons, and the way they winged across the night skies, hunting for sinners – children especially – to take back to their lairs in the moon. Paddy and I had laughed about it after he'd gone, over our bed-time milk and biscuits.

'There's all manner of things happen,' Mother Ryan said, holding me close, 'over on the mainland. We know little about them, nor need to. They've nought to do with the Western Isles. There's no cause to fear Demons here. You know, that, Ben, you know it well.'

She must have stayed with me till I fell asleep. Wide-awake in daylight, I writhed at the thought. If the noise I'd made had been loud enough to rouse her, Paddy might have heard it too. And Antonia. I visualized the little twist that lifted a corner of Antonia's mouth when she was hiding a smile; or pretending to.

Paddy and Antonia were Mother Ryan's daughters – no kin to me but, since I had lived with them all my life, almost like sisters. Elder sisters: Paddy by eighteen months, Antonia more than four years. Antonia was tall and thin, with fair hair that until recently had been kept tied back in a bun but was now let down, falling to the middle of her back. She had sharp grey eyes, quick and impatient movements. When she was angry it was in a held-back way more alarming than Mother Ryan's hot bursts of temper.

I doubt if anyone would have taken her and Paddy for sisters. Paddy was more sturdily built and ruddier; she had blue eyes, thick black hair cut short, and a much greater inclination to talk and laughter. We fought quite a lot because she had a bossy streak, but did nearly everything together. I could not imagine life without her; though for that matter it was impossible to imagine life without any of the people among whom I had grown up – Mother Ryan, Antonia, Andy and Joe, even the remote forbidding figure of the Master.

That morning, after we had our own breakfast, Paddy and I went down to the little paddock to give Jiminy his. Jiminy was a horse, sway-backed and nearly blind, who had been put out to grass. We took him his favourite snack – a sandwich with jam from last summer's plums – and he performed his usual trick of whinnying when he saw us coming, then backing away and circling before returning to the fence, yellow teeth bared in a greedy grin.

3

We went through the routine of feeding him and stroking his still velvety muzzle, but it wasn't the same. There had been an awkwardness over breakfast, and it persisted. Eventually I moved away towards Lookout, the highest point on the island, with Paddy following. Apart from a bank of cloud far off in the east and a few small clouds on the western horizon, the sky was blue, the air warm and carrying scents of spring.

From Lookout one could see all the other islands. Sheriff's, the only one with more than two score inhabitants, lay south-east across the central bay. John's and Stony were to our left; to our right, Sheep Isle and West Rock and January completed the ragged arc. Some of the names were self-explanatory: Stony was stony indeed, the green turf of Sheep was studded with white shapes, and it was from Sheriff's that Sheriff Wilson governed all the isles except the one on which we stood. This was Old Isle – I didn't know why except that it had a ruin much older than those on Sheriff's, which we knew were left over from the Madness. It was built with stones that bore the marks of hundreds, perhaps thousands of years of weathering.

We had explored all the islands, summer by summer. At one time we had been obliged to rely on Joe to take us, but since the previous spring we'd had the use of a small dinghy and could, with Mother Ryan's permission, roam freely. We had planned to camp a night on John's during the coming weekend.

Paddy chattered while we looked out – about when Liza, the tortoiseshell cat, might have her kittens, about Bob Merriton who had come over from January to court Antonia but been quickly mocked into a shame-faced retreat . . . about the school of seals Joe said had come into the bay on the far side of Stony . . . But her chatter had an uncertain note, and as is likely to happen with people who

4

are using words to fill an awkwardness, in the end she ran out of them. The silence that followed was heavy. She broke it with a yawn.

'I don't know why I feel tired. I slept like a log last night.'

The yawn was too obvious, but I would have known she was lying anyway: and why. I said curtly:

'Better go back to bed, in that case.'

I walked away, but she came after me. 'I'm sorry, Ben.'

'What about?'

She was silent again, but continued to follow as I walked down the hill. At last she said:

'*I* get frightened, when I think about them. I know there aren't any here, but that's not to say they might not come one day. There's no telling how far they can fly.'

I swung round to face her. 'So you did hear me yelling, in the night!' She made a movement of her head that could have been a shake or a nod. 'It was a nightmare, that's all. Anyone can have a nightmare.'

It was definitely a nod this time. 'I know.'

'When I'm awake I'm not scared of them.'

'Well, I am. I'm glad we live where there aren't any.'

I knew she was trying to make things right, and while I still nourished resentment was happier. However much we fought, I could be sure of Paddy being basically on my side. And there was some relief in having it in the open.

I said: 'I wonder *why* they don't come here. Perhaps they can't fly over water.'

'Mother said they had them in Ireland, and that's across water from the rest of the mainland. Maybe they don't think there's anything in the Isles that needs punishing.' She thought about that. 'Or perhaps we're too far off, too unimportant.'

'Or they're scared of the Master.'

Paddy laughed, but it wasn't entirely a joke. It was hard to imagine even Demons taking on the Master. We had come to the ruins and a couple of early butterflies – clouded yellows – waltzed overhead, spiralling up .past a pillar of crumbling grey stone.

'Do you want to talk about it,' Paddy asked, '– the nightmare?'

'No.'

I was certain of that. Discussing Demons in an abstract way was one thing: I couldn't begin to talk about the howling and my impotent panic. Awkwardness started to come back. Paddy said:

'I was thinking . . .'

'What?'

'Liza's kittens – she had her last litter in the old pigsty. I wonder if she's gone back there?'

I said more cheerfully: 'She might have. We could go and look.'

Later that day Andy brought me disturbing news: I was to accompany the Master on his customary afternoon ride around the island.

On my previous birthday, the Master had surprised me by giving me a present, in the shape of a pony. He had not previously marked such occasions, for any of us. There always was a present which was supposed to be from the Master, but we knew Mother Ryan had made it or got it from Sheriff's and wrapped it up before putting the Master's seal on it.

And a pony was something special. Joe had brought it across secretly the night before, but the Master himself summoned me to the paddock and handed me the reins. He didn't say much, only: 'So you're fourteen, boy. On the mainland, they would call you a man'. Then, without waiting for thanks to emerge from stammering confusion, he turned and walked away.

Antonia had just been scornful; for two or three days afterwards she greeted me by dropping her voice and saying: 'On the mainland, they would call you a man'. I don't think she minded my being given the horse; she was not fond of animals and shooed the cats away if they ventured into the parlour.

Paddy though had been resentful at first, pointing out that all she'd had for becoming fourteen was a new hat. But she got over it quickly, principally by treating the pony as if it were a present for the pair of us. It was she who provided him with a name, Black Prince, and when Andy taught us to ride him she learned faster. She was older, of course.

The Master's own horse was a big grey gelding named Sea King. Andy called him wilful, but he seemed docile with the Master's hands on the reins. I had only looked on from a respectful distance, and found it hard to take in Andy's instruction that I was to join him.

'Join him, how? Walk alongside?'

'On Black Prince, fool.' Andy pushed up the quiff of hair which disguised a bald patch on the top of his head. 'And mind you don't discredit me by riding like a sack of seaweed.' He grinned unpleasantly. 'Else I might send the Demons after you again.'

The direction was for meeting at North Point. As I came up to him, I said: 'Good day, Master', and put a hand to my fore-lock. He nodded silently, and clicked his tongue for Sea King to walk on.

For several hundred metres the path lay inland, before emerging to where the sea lay directly beneath us. He halted there. The western cloud had thickened, but the day was mild still.

The Master spoke abruptly. 'That was a fine caterwauling you treated us to last night.'

I was thrown once more into confusion. The Master's quarters were at the far end of the house, and it had not occurred to me he too might have been wakened.

'I'm sorry, sir . . .'

He stared down at me: he was more than two metres tall, his horse better than seventeen hands to Black Prince's thirteen and a half. Letting go the reins, he rubbed his hands together slowly.

'You have put on some height in the past year. How much?'

I had no trouble answering that. At the foot of the back stairs, pencil lines on the plaster marked where Paddy and I measured one another, regularly on birthdays and quite often in between.

'Eight centimetres, sir. Well, above seven.'

He nodded. 'Are you happy here?'

His voice was deep, and his manner of speaking strange. As Mother Ryan's was; but in her case we knew the reason – she was proud of being born and raised in Ireland. The Master's accent did not resemble either hers or the local one, which was also my own. It took me a moment to grasp the question, and 'here' perplexed me. Where else should I be? I said quickly:

'Yes indeed, sir.'

'It's a small place, for a growing boy. You have wanted education.'

Again I was puzzled. This was the spring holiday, but normally Paddy and I were taken daily to school on Sheriff's in Joe's fishing dinghy.

I said: 'I was second to top in my reading class. And Roger Burton who came top is six months older.'

He smiled, but his smile was bleak. 'And what do you read, in that class you speak of?'

8

'All sorts of things. "Duties and Obediences", "The Torments of Hell", "The Infidels of the North" . . .'

'Would you say you learn matters of value from these books?'

An honest answer would have been very little if anything; but I knew better than to be strictly honest to a questioning adult, particularly to the Master.

'Yes, sir.'

'I am told you dreamt of Demons last night. Do the books tell you of them?'

I nodded. 'Yes, they do.'

'What do they say?'

He sounded as though he really wanted to know, which in itself surprised me. I had taken it for granted that, with a large room lined ceiling to floor with books, he must be the wisest person I knew – far wiser than our teachers, or Mr Hawkins the Summoner, or Sheriff Wilson. But he had put the question, and I had better answer it.

'They tell us Demons are the minions of the Dark One. They come to warn men against transgression of the laws, and to punish those who persist in wickedness.'

He looked at me until I felt uncomfortable. At last, he said:

'I have served you ill.'

That puzzled me even more. How could the Master serve me, or want to? I kept silent, and he went on:

'It may not be too late. We will talk again, perhaps of Demons. Now it is time for your tea.'

I followed him back on Black Prince, disturbed but intrigued. Would the talk be in his library? I had ventured there once while he was away on Sheriff's, and the close-packed volumes had fascinated me. There was even a set of wooden steps, spiralling around a pole, to get at those too high to reach. Mother Ryan had caught me peering, and pulled me away by the ear. It was, she scolded with a sharp tweak, a spot forbidden to any but the Master.

All this took place on Tuesday. The new term started on Friday, which meant just one day before the weekend break. I had my fingers crossed for our camping trip: the weather had broken, and Mother Ryan fastened our oil-skins on a rain-smeared morning. Joe greeted us at the jetty.

'You're late. That's a bad beginning to the term.'

'No more than five minutes,' Paddy said. 'Liza had her kittens in the night. Joe, she's got *five*, and we saw the last one born! Two black-and-white, two tortoiseshell, and one a funny grey colour. We're calling it Smoky.'

That had been my suggestion. It was usually Paddy who thought of names, always Paddy who decided what the name was going to be.

Joe said: 'Never mind cats and kittens. Cast off, Ben. I've done a day's work before you were stirring, and an-other's waiting.'

The dinghy smelt of the catch he had landed earlier, a tang of fish mixed with salt and sweat and tobacco. Joe was almost as tall as the Master, and broader, with a bat-tered face and a big nose and thick black beard. He set sail to catch the stiff north-westerly, and we heaved our way across the bay with gusts of rain stinging our faces. I glanced surreptitiously at Paddy. I had got over being sea-sick, but she still suffered occasionally. She seemed all right this morning.

I looked back towards the house, where smoke rose from two small chimneys at the north end and a larger one at the south. The Master would be sitting by his study fire, drinking the coffee Mother Ryan took him about this time. I'd never tasted coffee – it was not for the likes of us,

Mother Ryan said – but loved the smell. Perhaps he would be reading one of his thousands of books. I wondered when the summons for the talk might come.

This being the first day of school, Sheriff Wilson addressed us. He reminded us of our duty: to obey our parents and those in authority, all adults, in word and deed and thought. We were to work hard and to learn – learn especially those things through which we might escape the wrath of the Dark One, in this life and the life to come. Work hard, and learn well!

He too was big, but fleshy. He had a high forehead, fat cheeks, and spectacles whose lenses had no rims. He picked me out as I headed towards the class-room.

'Young Ben of Old Isle! How are you, boy?'

'Well, sir. Thank you, sir.'

He was smiling, but he smiled easily. People said he was the best Sheriff in living memory, more easy-going than his predecessors. The stocks which stood across the green from his house were empty more often than not. I thought I ought to like him, but could not.

'The Master is well, I hope?'

The tone was solicitous, but I didn't believe the hope was honest. I had once observed him in conversation with the Master, and though I could not distinguish their words there had been contempt in the Master's voice, wheedling unease in the Sheriff's.

I said: 'He is well, sir.'

'Respect him, boy. He is a great man.'

'Indeed he is!'

I spoke warmly, and thought his eyes narrowed behind the rimless lenses; but he smiled still more widely, and patted my head to send me on my way.

Although I would not have preferred to live there, I found

Sheriff's an exciting place. Apart from ruinous mounds from the days of the Madness, fascinating forbidden territory, there was the bustle of people; and there were shops. The *Hesperus*, which took produce to the mainland and brought back other goods, had recently returned. Paddy and I found mainland sweets tastier than the Widow Barnes' fudge, and with hoarded pennies bought sticks of toffee studded with hazelnuts. We munched our way happily to the quay where Joe was waiting for us.

I began to rattle off an account of the day, but Paddy interrupted.

'What is it, Joe? What's wrong?'

When I looked, his expression was troubled. He turned his head away.

'Nothing that won't wait. We've a tide to catch.'

She grasped his arm. 'Tell us now.'

I envied her manner of commanding him. He stared unhappily. 'Well, you'll have to know. It's the Master.'

'What about him?' I asked.

But Paddy had read Joe's face. 'Not *dead?*'

'No,' I said. 'That can't be!'

Yet now I could read his grimness too, and knew it was.

2

We were subdued on the journey back to Old Isle. Halfway there, Joe was hailed by a ferryman from January.

'Is it true then?'

Joe merely nodded across the slop of waves and did not heave to: normally in mid-channel encounters boats grappled for five or ten minutes' gossip. We remained silent as the island loomed, the house outlined against a cloudy sunset. No smoke rose from the big chimney.

Mother Ryan, on the other hand, was voluble, scolding Paddy for a stain on her dress. I supposed she would round on me too, because I had a bigger one on my shirt and finger-tips inked blue; but she did not. Her voice seemed shriller than usual.

I'd thought Paddy might suggest going to see the kittens, but she disappeared upstairs. I considered visiting the old pigsty on my own, but couldn't make up my mind to it, to anything. I felt unsettled and uncertain. Memory summoned a picture from one of the books at school: of Death in a black cowl, brandishing a reaping hook at cowering mortals. I could not imagine the Master cowering; but he was dead.

My teacher had set work for the weekend, but I didn't feel like tackling that either. Would we be going to school on Monday, anyway? I drifted aimlessly; it seemed a long time before we were called to supper. As I came from the wash-house, Andy was approaching, spade in hand. At the far end of the garden, a little space behind a hedge of yews, enclosed by a knee-high wooden fence, was the island's graveyard. It held three headstones and half a dozen wooden markers. Andy wiped the spade clean and put it in the woodshed, but did not speak.

We took our places round the kitchen table, Antonia arriving last, paler than ever and walking as though each step was an effort. It was getting dark: the oil lamp on the sideboard had already been lit and Paddy brought one for the table as Mother Ryan carried in the soup tureen. I saw the faces etched in the yellow glow, and wondered if my own looked as strange.

I had a feeling it might not be proper to eat heartily, but nonetheless cleaned my plate of both soup and the stew that followed. Mother Ryan had fallen silent, and it was a quiet meal. When Joe, always the last to finish, put down his knife and fork, I looked across at Paddy.

It was established practice that she and I cleared away the dishes, and washed and dried them. At that time also Mother Ryan and Antonia would leave the table, one to prepare the tray with the Master's meal (including a silver jug of wine instead of Joe's and Andy's pots of ale), the other to carry it to his quarters. Tonight they sat on in silence, Mother Ryan staring at the lamp where a moth fluttered, Antonia looking into her lap.

At last Mother Ryan turned to Paddy. 'The dishes . . .' I got to my feet. 'Not you, Ben. Paddy will see to them.'

I sat down again. Paddy said: 'Why? Why *not* Ben?'

'Do as I say.'

'But it's not fair . . .'

'Patricia!'

Mother Ryan was plump and not tall, so it wasn't easy for her to look imposing; but when her voice took on its present note she was not to be trifled with. Nor when she called Paddy 'Patricia'. (Antonia was always Antonia; one could not imagine her with a nickname.)

Paddy rose reluctantly; and I followed suit. Whatever was going on, I preferred sharing the chore to incurring Paddy's resentment. I said:

'I don't mind helping.'

Mother Ryan shook her head. 'It wouldn't be proper.'

That made no sense. Joe and Andy drained their pots. It was Antonia who spoke.

'I don't see why he shouldn't.'

Their looks met, Mother Ryan's face not angry now, but troubled.

'You know – that there's a difference to be taken account of, matters to be explained.'

'Explain them, then. But until you do, nothing's changed. Let him help clear.'

Joe stood up, towering over us. 'All that which is necessary – has it been done?'

'Yes.' Mother Ryan's voice was steadier. 'I have seen to it myself.'

'Then I will pay respects.'

He made for the hall, Andy following. Mother Ryan said: 'We should all pay respects. Leave the dishes for now, Paddy. Come, Ben.'

The kitchen hall opened into a corridor that linked the two parts of the house. This end was lit by the lamps behind us; at the far end a wall lamp shone on the heavy oak door through which I had rarely dared venture. The corridor was hung with pictures of ships. Some displayed sails, billowing white against blue skies or reefed under stormy skies. Others were engined, but far more impressive than the *Hesperus*. One was a two-funnelled vessel of such a size – if those dots on the deck were people – that a score of ships like the *Hesperus* would fit inside it.

Joe pushed open the door. Here another hall, bigger and more elegant than ours, had lamps suspended behind crystal fingers which multiplied their light. In a high window to the right, coloured glass portrayed another sailing ship against a crimson sunset.

A second door led to the Master's dining room, whose central feature was a long mahogany table which would normally have been covered by a damask table-cloth. Now the polished wood bore an open coffin, on which a lamp shone down.

The Master lay in his shroud, hands folded across his chest. His long white face looked as if it were made of wrinkled paper rather than flesh. There were pennies on his eyes, gold coins atop the pennies. I stared at the folded hands. I had always marvelled at the immaculateness of his nails, my own being short and usually engrained with dirt: in death they looked still longer and finer.

Standing before the coffin, head bowed, Joe spoke in a clear voice. 'Duties and respects, Master. God be wi' ye; and all Demons absent.'

He bowed deeper, and turned away. Andy repeated the ceremony, as did the others: Antonia's voice broke, and she could not finish. When Paddy had done, I whispered:

'Shall I go?'

Mother Ryan nodded. 'Yes, Ben. It's your turn.'

I stared at the Master's body, finding nothing fearful but nothing which made me want to linger over the looking. I spoke, gabbling: 'Duties and respects, Master. God be with you and all Demons absent.' I turned to go, but Mother Ryan's voice halted me.

'There's more, Ben. From you.'

'More?'

'The duty of a son.' She looked flustered, and all their eyes were on me. 'Kiss your father.'

'What?' I stepped back from the coffin. 'That is *the Master*.'

Mother Ryan came forward, but stopped before she reached me. She stood with folded hands, as I had seen her stand in the Master's presence.

'He was, but is no longer. Kiss your father, Ben.'

That night the weather was wild, waking me to a rattle of windows, but it was a spring storm which pummelled the islands and moved quickly on. The Sheriff had sent word the funeral was not to be delayed, and late in the morning the sun shone as Andy and Joe bore the coffin to the grave, with rain-drops still scattering from the branches of trees under which they passed. Sheriff Wilson wore a black cloak instead of the crimson one which was his normal badge of office. The gaunt face of Mr Hawkins, the Summoner, looked even thinner and more miserable under a black pointed hat.

Sea-birds wheeled and shrieked overhead as the Summoner sought mercy from the Dark One for the Master's soul, and adjured all Demons that might hinder its passage to keep their distance. Paddy twisted a button of her dress, and Antonia stared at the raw, gashed earth as though hoping it might swallow her up too. She was not crying, but she never did. At her side, Mother Ryan wept enough for both.

After I had cast the first clod we trudged back to the house, leaving Andy and Joe to fill the grave. Mother Ryan was quiet now, though red-eyed. She and the girls had been up since dawn preparing the funeral meal, and there was hot punch laced with brandy for the men. Sheriff Wilson raised no objection when she poured an extra measure of spirits into his cup. Pushing up his spectacles, he looked searchingly at me, but spoke to her.

'You are sure the boy inherits? His parentage is certain?'

'I am sure.'

'Yet nothing was ever said of this. The Master did not speak of it to me.'

'It was his wish it should not be spoken of, even to the boy. Those of us who came here with him knew of it.'

He clicked his tongue, shaking his head. 'There should be documents.'

'As indeed there are, your Honour.'

She fetched a blue and white vase from the sideboard and shook out papers which she handed to the Sheriff.

'He bade me take care of them. There are marriage lines, and his Will. I witnessed that myself.'

'Yet the boy knew nothing?'

He looked at me fiercely. I thought again of the good reports that were made of him, and believed them even less. I would not care to be at his mercy. His voice was incredulous too, but I could scarcely blame him for that. Since the previous evening I had thought of little else, but still could scarcely believe what I had been told. He examined the papers closely.

'The marriage took place in Ireland?'

'It did, and I was present at it.'

He said, very reluctantly: 'They seem to be in order.'

'All things concerning the Master were in order.'

He put the papers down and turned to me. Now he was smiling, but I didn't trust the smile.

'So, Ben! This is a considerable inheritance, especially for a boy still at school. You will need guidance.'

I said 'Yes, sir' obediently, without meaning it. Though hard to credit, the knowledge that Old Isle belonged to me was something to hug close. And while I would not have wished him dead to gain it, the Master had done little to make me mourn him. Receiving none, I had felt neither

18

love nor even affection for him. Respect, yes, but that induced no sense of loss. As for my undreamed-of inheritance, I had not yet had time to think what to do with it but was determined it would be in my own way. For the present, for some years even, I might have to defer to the Sheriff, but wishes were horses now. I would school mine privately.

'How did he come to die . . .' – I hesitated before uttering the word – '. . . my father?'

The Sheriff's party had gone back, after the Sheriff had firmly told us it would be school as usual on Monday, and Andy and Joe had returned to their everyday business. Antonia, once the clearing was done, had retired to her room; I didn't know where Paddy was. I sat on the shiny black horse-hair sofa in Mother Ryan's parlour, beneath the ponderously ticking wall clock, watching her darn socks. She had finished mending the heel of one of mine and picked up another, only to drop it. It had been the Master's, woven not of wool but soft silk. Would I wear such, I wondered?

'It began with a pain in his head.' She found another sock and held it to the light. 'He spoke of it when I took him his morning tea. I knew it could be no trivial matter, for he was not a man to complain of aches. I said he should get Joe to take him to the physician on Sheriff's, but he would have none of it. After you'd gone to school, it worsened. Soon he knew he was going, and spoke of you and what needed to be done. He died just on noon.'

'What else did he say?'

'Things I mostly didn't understand . . . of people and places that signified nothing to me. The misery in his head likely made him ramble.' She paused. 'And he spoke of your mother.'

'What of her?'

'Only such as would have no meaning to you – to anyone living but me.'

I sensed reluctance, and pressed her. 'Tell me about her.'

She hesitated. 'You'll not understand the way it was. She and I were girls together, as close as two could be till I was married. And still close, after that. Then the Master came to our village, a tiny place with no town nearer than ten miles. We knew nought of him; except he was old, and had money. He bought the castle that stood above the village, and the both of us went in service to him there.

'He was a man on his own – and lonely. That was the reason for his marrying your mother: being alone and in need of a wife. She knew the way it was. Her father was keen on her marrying this rich old foreigner and she did as she was bid. It was out of duty, not fondness.

'The fondness did not come till after, with both of them, but ah, it was strong! Even more on his side than hers – he lived for the sight and sound of her. She could never fathom the reason – she being a country girl and him a grandee from no one knew where – but it was not to be doubted. And then she loved him back with all her heart, especially after you were born.'

It was troubling to listen to such a story, and know it was a part of my own. Mother Ryan fell silent. I asked:

'How did she die?'

'It's all over and done with, long since.' The reluctance was plain again. 'It's enough having the day's sorrows to endure, without calling back yesterday's.'

'I want to know.'

'It can do no good.'

'I'm entitled to know.' I was almost angry with her. 'Tell me.'

She shook her head, but said: 'It was a sad bad business.

At the Summonings, things were said: that the castle was an unholy place, the Master himself a cause of offence to the Dark One. He laughed when he was told of it, saying he had no fear of Demons – mocking them.

'Even for him, it was folly. At the next Summoning, a curse was put on him. That night the Demons danced, and people came up from the village, and there was shouting at the castle gate. He had no fear still, but went out to them, defying them and Demons both, and they durstn't assail him to his face. But while he was rebuking their insolence, some sneaked round the back with faggots and put a torch to the building.

'The castle was an old place, mostly wood, and that was a dry summer. It flared in minutes, and the sky was lit with the flames. Your mother died that night; and so did the father of Antonia and Paddy, trying to save her. The Master managed to get to you in your cot and bring you out. It took three men to hold him from going back into the fire for her, though the flames were leaping higher than the tower.'

My initial questioning had been provoked by the death of a man I had feared and respected but never known, and had produced a predictable answer – that he had died in a way old men might reckon to die. My mother had never been more than a shadowy figure, arousing no curiosity: in every way that mattered Mother Ryan had been my mother. Now, shockingly, my natural mother had gained identity, an identity lit by romance but shadowed with horror. To die in such a way . . .

'After it, he could not abide staying there,' Mother Ryan said. 'And I was left with two small children, and no man. The Master brought us all here, to the islands. For above two years he did not look at you, and afterwards was distant, bidding me keep you as my own.' She shook her head, smiling. 'That was no hard thing. But it was not

21

through want of love, you understand – had he not carried you out of the fire, with burning timbers falling round him? Maybe it was through too much. He saw her again in you, and scarce could bear it.'

I realized she was trying to soften things for me, but it did not help. Yet it was I who had insisted on an answer, and no one's fault if I had been given more than I bargained for. The clock ticked heavily, the kettle whistled softly on the hob; and in my mind flames roared. I stood up.

'The kettle's on the boil,' Mother Ryan said. 'I'll brew us some tea.'

I shook my head; even the grate's tame fire repelled me. 'I'm going out.'

'Before you do . . . there's a thing he had. I don't know what it is, or where it came from, but he wore it next to his skin. I took it from him when I laid him out.'

She went to a drawer in the sideboard which housed her treasures: old letters tied with faded green ribbon, a drawing of a young man smiling, a tortoiseshell comb. She returned carrying a gold chain which bore a medallion. I wondered, as I took it from her, if it might be a locket with a picture of my mother.

But if it was a locket, I could see no way of opening it. The medallion was a disk of smooth grey material, with a silvery design worked into the surface. It was plainly very hard, the design complex and meaningless, full of curves and squiggles. I did not think it had anything to do with my mother: more likely it was something left over from the Master's unknown life before he met her. Unknown, and now for ever unknowable.

I felt I had had enough of mysteries, and questions. I was tempted to hand it back to her, but that would have been ungracious. Her eyes were on me, pleased with having saved it for me.

So I slipped the chain over my neck. The medallion felt strange against my chest, cool at first but soon warm. This was the way the Master had worn it, but it did not make me feel like a Master.

John's was no more than three hundred metres square, and uninhabited. It lacked a spring, so we took water in a can. That was for drinking and cooking – we had an ocean to wash in.

After my talk with Mother Ryan I had not much wanted to go on the expedition: in any case, with Saturday lost, we could not stay overnight. But when Paddy woke me early, and I expressed some doubt, her voice turned waspish.

'I suppose you'd rather sit and make a list of your possessions – count your gold pieces, maybe. Don't worry. I'll get Joe to take me over.'

She was halfway down the stairs by the time I could get out of bed, but relented enough to agree to wait while I washed and dressed. She remained stiff and distant for a time after that, but by the time we had wrestled our gear onto the dinghy was her usual self. We had left a house silent in the sharp light of dawn, with no smoke yet rising from the kitchen chimney. I wondered about the chimney at the far end – whether Mother Ryan would still light a fire in the Master's quarters. In my quarters, I thought, and shot a guilty look at Paddy in case she read my mind.

The sea was quiet as the morning while we rowed the few hundred metres to John's. Gulls bobbed on the water and I saw a cormorant leisurely paddling, too lazy or too sated to dive for fish. The island's single beach was on the far side, looking across waters empty to the western horizon. The tide was nearly full, but we still dragged the dinghy higher after beaching it. Then we set about building a fire and cooking breakfast.

We had brought porridge which had been all night on the stove and only needed re-heating, but there were bacon and sausages to grill and eggs to fry. Paddy automatically resumed her role of bossing me – telling me the bacon was not crisp enough, chiding me for breaking the yolk of her egg. But she ate as greedily as I: food tasted better cooked over a fire we had made ourselves, on an island whose sole occupants we were. Behind us the sun was obscured by the rise of land, but the sea in front was already brightly lit.

Lying back on the sand, face hidden as she laced hands behind her neck, Paddy spoke of my new status.

'Was it *really* a surprise? Did Mother never give you a hint of it – nor the Master, either?'

'None at all.'

'I knew nothing, but Antonia must have. There were things she said which make sense now. I think she remembers quite a bit from the time before we came here.'

Paddy started talking about things that could be done on Old Isle. Sheriff Wilson's house had a pool, which was connected to the sea and held water at low tide. We might make one like it. He kept fish for the table in his. We could swim in ours when the sea was rough.

I pointed out it would mean digging a very long channel, since the Master's house was at least twice as far from the shore. It would be asking a lot of Andy and Joe.

'We can bring men over from Sheriff's. And they could build a summer-house, up by the pines.'

My latest acquisition seemed destined to go the same way as the previous one: to be shared between us, but with Paddy in charge. I wondered if she would want to ride Sea King. Probably not; his size would be likely to daunt even her. Anyway, for the last couple of days he had been suffering an attack of laminitis, and was confined to stables.

The day passed quickly. We put to rights a tree-house in

the island's little copse, which Joe had helped us build on a previous visit, and searched for gulls' eggs on the rocky ribs of the foreshore where they nested. By the time we'd collected a dozen we were hungry again, and made a new fire and boiled them, burning our fingers as we cracked the shells to eat them with salt and butter.

A mile or so out, someone was lifting lobster pots. There was a reef there where Joe put down pots, but this was not his boat. It was bigger – someone from Sheriff's probably. Yet so tiny compared with the vessel in the picture. I asked idly:

'Why did things get small?'

'Gull's eggs? I don't recall them being bigger. Not much fun for the gull, if they were.'

'I meant boats. And buildings. Remember that ruin we explored on Sheriff's . . .'

'Not for long, because you were scared of being caught in a forbidden place.'

As I recalled it, she had been at least as scared, but I didn't argue. I said:

'That book we found which could still be read – with pictures of buildings ten times as high as the Sheriff's house.' I thought about it. 'Twenty times, perhaps.'

'It wasn't that they got small: the Demons destroyed them. It says so in 'Laws of the Dark One' – that the Demons will destroy anything built more than six times the height of a man, and lay waste the ground as far all round it. Except for windmills.'

'But why? What's wrong about tall buildings, or big boats?'

'It's wrong if the Dark One says it's wrong. You know that. Windmills are allowed for the Demons, so they can perch on the sails. It's to do with what happened long ago – with the Madness.'

'Then what *was* the Madness?'

25

'It's not to be talked of. You know that, too.'

I knew it, but I didn't know why. 'It wasn't just build-ings. There were pictures of enormous machines as well.'

'They probably weren't real.'

'They looked real. And there was that picture of a big machine in a rocky desert place, with words underneath: "The first men on the Moon".'

Paddy laughed. 'Doesn't that prove they weren't real, you noodle? The Moon's where the Demons live. How could anyone get there?'

What she said was unanswerable, but unsatisfying. The very oldness of the book, the crumbling brown-edged pages stained with damp and smelling of must, had worked powerfully on my imagination, and still did when I thought of it. Men and women, people like us, had written those words, drawn those strange disturbing pictures. And drawn them with a faithfulness and clarity that even Miss Phipps, our Art teacher, could not have begun to match. What reason would they have for lying?

But I could not properly express my doubts, and knew this was forbidden territory. I retreated to an earlier point. 'I've never seen a Demon perching on the mill on Sheriff. Have you?'

'Well, you don't want them to, do you?'

That was true enough, but didn't seem to have much to do with tall buildings, or anything else. I shrugged, dismiss-ing it firmly from my mind, and peeled another egg.

We went swimming, not for long because the water still had its winter chill, and basked as the sun dropped towards the line where blue met blue. I heard a distant rumble which sounded like thunder but dismissed it as fancy: there wasn't a cloud in the sky. Paddy said:

'We could have stayed the night. The weather looks set fair.'

'Mother wouldn't allow it, with school tomorrow.'

'She couldn't stop us, could she? No one can tell you what you must do.'

'You' meant 'us'. 'Anyway, there *is* school. Sheriff Wilson said.'

'And who's Sheriff Wilson, to tell the Master of Old Isle what to do about *school*?'

We wrangled, talking pleasant nonsense. Seagulls screamed off-shore, before settling among the rocks, perhaps to lay more eggs. Time drifted past. Then Paddy said:

'What's that?'

'What?'

She pointed. Beyond the island's shoulder, black smoke rose against the blue. 'A fire . . .'

'Menhennick's haystack, most likely.'

He was a farmer on Sheriff's who had twice been fined for letting his hay catch fire, and threatened with the stocks if it happened again.

'At this time of year?' That was a point: his stack would be near exhausted. 'And it's not the right direction for Sheriff's.'

Rocks barred our way to the north, but there was a southern route to the far side of the island. We ran across rabbit-cropped grass, where ground-roses were budding, still only idly curious. We rounded the point, and Sheep Isle and January and Sheriff's in turn came into view, peaceful in afternoon sunshine.

And now we could see Old Isle; and it was from there the dark plume rose, billowing out of smoke that completely enveloped the house.

3

The smell reached us before we beached, but grew much stronger as we ran up the path beside the lower paddock. It was a reek of burning wood, mixed with less identifiable smells, now and then nauseating. The ruins of the house were capped by a dark cloud from which occasional flames still burst. I heard a snort from Jiminy, and saw him down by the bottom fence, as far away as he could get. Paddy was ahead, and I fought a stitch pelting after her.

We were halted by heat as we reached the monkey-puzzle tree on the front lawn. The whole of the far side was withered, the spiky branches wilting and charred. A few feet from where we stood the grass was burnt dark brown.

Paddy called out. 'Mother ... Antonia!' Her voice was shrill above the crackling grumble of the conflagration. I said:

'Perhaps if we get round to the other side ...'

We had to make a wide circuit. I saw Sea King and Black Prince standing together, over by the pea field, but no other sign of life. No sound either, except the growling of the fire and a startling crack as one of the remaining uprights collapsed: not even a bird. Paddy called again, her cheeks flushed from running and wet with tears.

'I'm sure they got out,' I said.

'Where are they, then?'

We stared at the scene of desolation, and the sight brought back the story I'd been told the previous night. I had always loved the comfort of flame in a kitchen grate, the thrill of it leaping above autumn bonfires. I'd never dreamed how much I could hate it.

Sea King neighed, and I turned to see him rear, perhaps stung by a fleck of hot ash.

'The horses!' I pointed to where the stables had been reduced to a separate smouldering heap. 'Sea King was being kept in, because of his leg. Someone let them out, and if there was time for that . . .'

'Then where are they?' Paddy asked, and I had no answer. It was she who said urgently: 'Joe's cottage!'

This was the only other habitation on Old Isle. It nestled in a dip, a couple of hundred metres from the house. It was tiny, with only two rooms and a doorway under which Joe must stoop to enter. The door stood open, and there was someone in Joe's rocking chair. With light from only one small window, it took a moment to recognize the figure: the quiff of hair identified Andy.

'Where's Mother,' Paddy demanded, '– and Antonia?'

He rocked, with hunched shoulders. 'Gone.' His voice was slurred. 'The house burnt to cinders, and all in it. Every last thing . . .'

Shaking him, Paddy dislodged a bottle which rolled across the floor. It sounded empty. He went on rocking, and rambling:

'It was the Demons, come in judgement. Out of the sky they came, in a flaming chariot. We ran out, and I hid my face from the sight of it. Then there was the sound of a hundred thunderclaps rolled into one, and the house was turned to a fiery furnace. And after that, with a roar and a whoosh, they'd gone.'

Paddy gripped his shoulders. 'Where *are* they?'

29

'How would I know where they went, or any man? On the wings of the wind, to the Moon and maybe beyond. To think I dared mock them, with tales to frighten children . . .'

He winced as her fingers dug in. 'I'm talking of Mother and Antonia. What happened to them?'

'Taken. Both taken.'

I whispered: 'By the Demons?'

Andy shook his head. 'No, they'd been and gone.'

'Then how?' Paddy shook him violently. '*Who took them*?'

'The Sheriff's men. He must have seen the fire and sent them over. It was they that took them away.'

Fresh air was welcome after the brandy fumes. I assumed we would head back to the dinghy, and said: 'We can get across before the tide turns. It won't be easy otherwise, with the wind from the south-east.'

She said: 'I don't know . . .'

'But it *is*.' I touched finger to tongue, and raised it. 'Almost due south-east.'

'About going to Sheriff's.'

'You heard what happened. The Demons burnt the house, but the Sheriff's men took Mother and Antonia. He's drunk, but not so drunk as to have made it up.'

'I don't know. We ought to talk to Joe.'

'He won't be back till after dark, if the mackerel are running well.'

'And there are things that need doing – the animals to see to.'

She was heading away from the jetty. I followed, arguing.

'I think we ought to go right away. We don't know why they've been taken to Sheriff's.'

30

'We know they're all right.'

'Do we?' I was irritated by her obstinacy. 'Do you care?'

She whirled on me. 'Who are you to talk about caring? It's *my* mother, and my sister. No kin to you, just as you're nothing to anyone. Not even to *him*, till after he was dead. He may have left you the island, but he wanted nothing to do with you while he was alive.'

The unfairness struck me to silence; as did the bitter truth in it. I had nothing to say, and followed her dumbly. But she was already regretting her words. Antonia, I always felt, believed anyone she wounded deserved to be hurt. Paddy wasn't like that. She stopped and turned round.

'Of *course* they'd be taken to Sheriff's. They took them so they could have food and shelter: there's nothing left here. They'd have taken Andy if he hadn't been hiding with a bottle.'

When I still didn't speak, she grabbed me into a hug. 'I'm sorry, Ben! I didn't mean it. Truly. But I think we'd best talk to Joe. It's a feeling.'

Mother Ryan was the one for feelings, and signs and omens — about things happening to people when she'd dreamed of them, or they'd been in her mind. She'd had Andy in her mind the time he fell out of the apple tree and broke a leg. And the cow she'd been thinking about the whole of a weekend dropped a dead calf on the Monday.

Feelings went with sayings: 'Wednesday's dream on Thursday told is bound to come true be it never so old' . . . 'Cross on the stair, the morrow beware' . . . 'Pass the salt, pass the sorrow' . . . (Woe betide anyone who failed to put the salt down firmly on the table, for the next person to pick up).

These were aspects of life I accepted without question, though with a degree of bewilderment. I never had such feelings myself. I hadn't known Paddy have them before either, but it was probably different for a girl.

31

The hug eased but did not banish the smart, and the truth of what she had said left a chill that lingered. I had not thought much about who I was, taking Mother Ryan's loving care and all that went with it for granted. In recent days there had been a succession of shocks: of discovering a father only after his death; of gaining an unexpected inheritance, and of seeing it reduced to ashes. I knew even less of who I was, but no longer felt content with ignorance.

But Paddy had been right about there being things to do. We settled the horses and Abel the donkey in the lower meadow, where a spring provided water, and filled hay-racks from the barn to supplement the young grass. The hen-house at the end of the kitchen garden had escaped the fire: we fed the hens and collected eggs. We made sure the cows had water, but left the milking to Andy. It might help sober him: he said the warmth of a cow's flank soothed an aching head.

We found Liza and her kittens safe and sound in a hollow tree. We had no food for her but she was a cunning hunter and one could be sure the rats had survived. Rats survive everything.

It was Paddy who spotted Joe's boat rounding Anchor Point, as Venus brightened in a darkening sky beside a pallid quarter moon. Before we went to meet him, I looked again at the heap of ashes which was all that was left of the only home I had known.

I thought of the Master's books, the polished table which had borne his coffin, the paintings of strange ships . . . dust among embers. All the Master's possessions – or mine, but I had not had time to take that in. With them had gone the few objects that really belonged to me: the catapult I'd meant to take to John's but left behind through Paddy hurrying me, the wooden sea-serpent Joe spent most of one winter carving. I had only one thing left: putting my hand in my shirt I touched the medallion. It offered no comfort; in the evening air the metal felt cold and strange against my flesh.

I felt better after listening to Joe. It was a pity about the house, but houses were only houses, and no one had been hurt. When Andy rambled about Demons, he shrugged. If they had been here they had also gone. He wrinkled a disapproving nose at the state of his cottage, and ordered Andy away to the pump to wash.

'The Master's brandy will have gone with the rest, and that's no bad thing. He can maybe cool his fancy without it. In the morning we'll go to Sheriff's and see what's to be done, but first there's supper to see to.'

'We've got eggs,' I said.

'And they'll do well for breakfast. But if you run down to the boat now, you can bring up half a dozen fat mackerel.'

For various reasons, we were late setting off next morning.

There was a set-to when Joe spoke of the cows, and Andy said he would see to them in his own good time. Previously both had taken instructions from Mother Ryan, on behalf of the Master. (Now presumably on my behalf, but I judged it wiser to ignore that). They needed to establish whose say counted in her absence. Andy, as the Master's groom and personal servant, had been part of the household, Joe just a fisherman and general helper. But it was Joe who prevailed, Andy who went off grumbling to do as he was told.

It was Joe also who got us hunting through the ruins to see if there was anything worth salvaging. We came away choking and soot-blackened, with little beyond pots and pans and some crockery and cutlery. Joe retrieved a metal statue of a man on horseback from what had been the Master's quarters. For want of a better idea, we set it up at the head of the Master's grave.

We cleaned ourselves up, and finally got away with the sun already high above Sheriff's hill. Wind filled the smack's sail, and there was a good following tide. I had a sense of putting things behind me, and of excitement as to what would come next. I was brought out of day-dreaming by Joe saying: 'Looks like they worked late loading last night.'

'What do you mean?' Paddy asked.

He braced an arm against the tiller, and pointed. 'The *Hesperus* yonder. She wasn't due to sail till the evening tide.'

The *Hesperus* was backing out of the little harbour, a haze of smoke blowing back across her bows. We watched as the distance between us shrank. By the time she had come out and swung round, the dots on deck had become people – crew working, others standing against the rail. I was aware of a tenseness in Paddy.

'Mother!'

I recognized them myself: both Mother Ryan and Antonia. They looked in our direction. Antonia called something, but her words were taken by the wind.

Paddy urged: 'Get in closer, Joe.'

He tried, but it was no use. The *Hesperus'* whistle sent seagulls shrieking into the sky, and water churned about her stern as the engines were set full speed ahead. The gap widened again. We called, but I knew they could not hear us as the *Hesperus* made for the open sea.

This was the first time I had been inside the Sheriff's house. From the window of the room where we waited, I could see Old Isle and the smudge that had been the

Master's house. In this building the ceilings were higher but there was no upstairs. Even the Sheriff's house must not rise more than six times the height of a man.

The walls here had paintings too, not of ships but of old men in red robes. Beneath each, gold letters spelled a name and figures told the years in which he had been Sheriff of the Western Isles. The picture of Sheriff Wilson displayed his customary smile, but he was not smiling as he entered the room.

'Ben,' he said, 'son of him who was Master of Old Isle.' He paused. 'There are matters that require consideration. Serious consideration.'

He paused, and Paddy broke in. She had learned nothing from the men who had brought us here, and her impatience got the better of her.

'We saw my mother and sister, on the *Hesperus*. Where have they gone? And why?'

The Sheriff frowned. 'In good time, girl.'

The forbidding figure of the Master apart, we had been accustomed to speaking pretty well as we pleased on Old Isle; but school had taught us that things were different on Sheriff's, where children did not speak before being spoken to and never interrupted an adult, much less someone as important as the Sheriff. I nudged Paddy hard, and she held her tongue. After a disapproving stare, the Sheriff turned back to me.

'It is your position, Ben, which is at issue. This supposed inheritance of yours needs looking into, but there's a more weighty matter. Demons burnt down the Master's house, within forty-eight hours of his death. The Summoner may have something to say on that account.'

I had no idea what he was talking about, but thought we were more likely to get information by buttering him up. I said, with as much deference as I could muster:

'Yes, sir. I know everything is being done properly and in order . . .' He pursed his lips, but looked more affable. 'But meanwhile . . .'

'Meanwhile what, boy?'

'Paddy's mother and sister . . .' I attempted an ingratiating smile. 'Could you tell us what's happening to them?'

He folded his arms, pushing out his belly. 'Have you studied the Statutes of the Western Isles?'

I wanted to say: no more than anyone has, apart from you and a few other moth-eaten fossils – but refrained. The Statutes were contained in huge volumes, bound in green leather, which took up the whole of a shelf in the court room above the Sheriff's chair. One would have been risking a sprained arm, getting one of them down.

'The Western Isles,' he went on, 'hold fast to their rights and customs. No outlander may dwell in them, except with the consent of Sheriff and Council. When Old Isle was bought by the one they called the Master, that consent was neither sought nor granted. It was before my time of office.'

A flicker of satisfaction accompanied that. I said:

'Yes, sir. I see, sir. But does it matter, now the Master's dead?'

'He brought other outlanders with him: Mrs Ryan, her two daughters, and you. With you, as I've said, there are special considerations. Mrs Ryan and her daughters are a different case. She and the elder daughter have been sent to the mainland, and from there I imagine will be sent on further to Ireland, the place they originally came from. Patricia will follow in due course.'

'But they've lived here for years!' I said. 'It's not fair.'

'We are not speaking of fairness, but of law which is more important.' He was so pleased with himself that he failed to rebuke my outburst. 'These islands have pride in their traditions, and will not tolerate their being flouted.'

I was tempted to say: the Master flouted them and you knew it – but you were afraid of him. I managed not to.

'Until the *Hesperus'* next trip,' the Sheriff said, 'Patricia will be lodged with the Widow Winnick. You, Ben, will remain in my custody.'

The time we had together was short and not cheerful. Paddy was miserable about the delay in getting to Sheriff's: if we'd made the trip yesterday, she would have been reunited with the others before they were sent away. In which case, I reflected, I would have been left here on my own.

Despite that depressing thought, I did what I could to improve her mood by speaking of the feeling she'd had which had made us put the trip off. I probably phrased it badly: she snapped back that I ought to try not to be such a know-it-all. And if it hadn't been for going to John's with me she would have been on Old Isle when it all happened. I refrained from pointing out it was she who'd pressed me into the expedition, but failed to mend matters. When the Sheriff's man came to take her away, she didn't say good-bye.

That evening the Sheriff took me to a special Summoning. The island hall was packed, with people crowding in at the door. Summoner Hawkins' thin face was grim, and his voice echoed harshly from the black-painted walls. He warned us of the penalties for impiety. Living remote from other lands as we did, we might reckon ourselves safe, protected by the sea; but in thinking thus we deceived ourselves. No place on earth, however small, however distant, escaped the eye of the Dark One, or the long strong arm of his chastisement.

There had been some who said Demons would never

come to the Western Isles – some so deeply sunk in folly as to whisper that there were no Demons. They knew better now! The Demons had sent fire out of the sky to annihilate this corrupted dwelling of an enemy of the Dark One. Let it stand as a warning to all. The Dark One was not mocked. His enemies would perish, as this one and all his goods had perished.

I listened, shocked. It was one thing to find that the Master's house had been destroyed by Demons, quite another to have it described as just retribution. Although he stood close by me, I noticed that the Sheriff avoided contact. The Summoner's anger was plain, and the congregation listened in an ominous silence. Paddy's face, even if set in the unfriendly lines I had last seen, would have been a welcome sight, but this was a Summoning to which only adults were admitted.

But in that case, why had I been brought?

Days of loneliness ensued. I sat at meals with the Sheriff, who ate in grim silence; much as I had mistrusted his smile, I would have been glad to see it back. At school I was moved to a desk set apart, and teachers only spoke to me to give curt instructions. None of the other pupils came near. When I caught sight of Paddy, she turned her head away.

Only now did I appreciate how carefree my old life had been. The Master may have been forbidding, but only as a figure in the background. My daily existence had been filled with warmth and affection. Losing that would have been bad enough, without the imposition of this friendless silence.

I slept at the back of the house, next to the bedroom of Joanna, the cook. I guessed I had been put there for her to keep an eye on me at night, though she slept so soundly, snoring like a dozen hedgehogs, that her surveillance was meaningless. But where could I escape to, on an island where I was known and shunned by all?

It was her snoring that caused me to fail at first to grasp the significance of the noise from the window. The second time, I recognized the clatter of gravel on glass and slipped out of bed. The night was windy, with a half moon dipping in and out of cloud; and I had no difficulty distinguishing the figure standing out there.

'Paddy!'

'We haven't time to talk.' Her whisper was fierce. 'Get dressed.'

'I'm forbidden to go out without a guard.' Joy at seeing her was dashed by recollection of my plight. 'There's no-where to go, anyway. It'll only mean more trouble – for you, too.'

Her voice was impatient. 'Do you realize how much trouble you're in, as it is?'

'Of course I do.'

'No, you don't. No one talks to you, so you don't know what's being said.'

'I was at the Summoning. I heard Summoner Hawkins say the Demons burnt the house because the Master was an enemy of the Dark One. But that was the Master, and he's dead.'

'It's not all they're saying. They say it was because of the Master the Demons came; and they also say they'll come back unless something's done, and this time lay waste to the islands.'

In the next room, Joanna's snoring paused but resumed in a higher key. I felt a chill.

'Unless what's done?'

'Unless they rid themselves completely of the Demons' bane. That means you.'

I could guess how: the Demons relished a burning. I said, with a quiver:

'There's nowhere to go.'

'Joe has the boat ready.'

'They'll search the islands.'

'It doesn't matter. We're going to the mainland. Now, *hurry*.'

4

The fishing boats would go out on the dawn tide: we cast off with the town asleep under the moon. The breeze was stiff and from its usual westerly quarter. It took some tacking to clear the bay, but after that we had a clear run. By the time moonlight began to fade into the glow of day, Sheriff's was no more than a distant shadow, the other islands invisible behind it.

Joe produced bread and cheese and a flask of tea, which I tackled ravenously: freedom put an edge on appetite. Paddy, her face grey in the pallid light, would not even drink. We were out in the deep of ocean, with a swell under us that had built up over uncountable sea miles. The moon and the last dimming stars soared and dropped as we rolled from crest to trough and back. She would do better to be sick, I thought, and get it over.

Joe looked at her too, and perhaps by way of distraction started talking about people on the mainland. He had not been there often, and always been glad to get away. I asked why.

'It ain't easy to put words to it. They're mostly civil but . . . I don't know . . . closed in. I'd never be sure where I was with 'em. I'm not sure you're doing the right thing, travelling there.'

'We *have* to.' Paddy's voice was choked. 'They were going to send me anyway, as soon as the *Hesperus* gets back.'

'That's as may be, like most things folk worrit on. To-morrow comes is certain, but often as not it don't come the way you reckon.'

'They've already sent Mother and Antonia.'

'Which isn't to say they couldn't be brought home again. I've heard talk in the pubs – that people who've lived as long in the islands as they ought to be let stay. There's been mention of a petition to the Council.'

'And Ben? What kind of talk have you heard about him?'

It was a moment or two before he answered. 'Not such as one needs pay heed to. They was frit by what happened. They'd come to think they were safe from Demons out here. When a ten-year storm breaks, folks get scairt of the sea; but by next winter they've forgotten. They'll see things different as time goes by and nought happens.'

'Do *you* think nothing will happen, Joe,' I asked him, '– the Demons won't come back?'

I was hoping for reassurance. What Paddy had told me had gone deep. Being blackened by association with the Master was bad enough, but to be singled out as a target was really frightening. I would have liked to hear Joe dismiss that too.

And perhaps he would have, but at that moment Paddy abandoned her battle and lurched for the side of the boat. Joe thrust the tiller at me, and went to her. I listened to him comforting her as the sea's weight pressed against my straining arm. Over the sound of wind and waves I heard a distant honking, and looked up to see a long vee traversing the pale grey sky. Geese flying north; but they could as easily have been Demons.

From Sheriff's to the mainland's tip was forty kilometres, to our landfall twenty more. With the help of tide and

42

wind we made good time, and came into the bay late in the morning.

My notion of a port was the harbour at Sheriff's, where the *Hesperus* towered above the local dinghies and fishing smacks. I could see the *Hesperus* as we nosed in, but here she herself was dwarfed by a couple of ships three times her tonnage, and I saw more than half a dozen that matched her. Sheriff's town could have fitted inside this harbour, and above it an immensely bigger town stretched out. Immensely busier, too: with a slow-moving traffic of carts, carriages, horses and pack-donkeys.

Joe had brought us in near the seaward end of the quay. As he started to tie up, Paddy said: 'You go on back, Joe. We'll be all right now.'

Her colour had returned, and she spoke with her old authority. I was alarmed: it was unnerving to think of being left in a strange country among strange people. The town was intimidating enough, but beyond, I knew, stretched a land where one might walk for days, or weeks, without glimpsing broad water.

Joe simply grinned. 'How would I face Mother Ryan, if I did? Help me tie up, and we'll get started on finding them.' He scratched his beard. 'Though how to set about it may take some thinking.'

No one seemed to have noticed us, and no one paid attention as we made our way along the quay. One of the cargo ships was preparing to leave: it had steam up though the gangplank was still out. A few sailors were engaged in last-minute bargaining with traders who offered sweet-meats, hot pies and muffins, and a variety of trinkets. They cried their wares in what might have been a foreign language for all I could make of it, but there was nothing exotic in their appearance. The sailors mostly had blue jerseys with bright neck-bands and coloured caps, but the traders all wore dull browns and greys.

Joe said quietly: 'See along yonder?'

Through the press of people, I saw a barrier at the end of the quay. The bar itself was raised but two men in grey uniform with guns over their shoulders stood beside it.

'That's the check-point. They might ask questions.'

'And if they don't like the answers,' Paddy said, 'they might not let us through?'

'Or maybe take us in for more questioning. As I said, they're a funny lot. It could be a notion not to catch their attention in the first place.'

I asked: 'How?'

I didn't like the guns. Some in the islands had shotguns, but these looked different, more threatening. Joe said:

'We could dive in the harbour, and swim past.' For a moment I thought he was serious. 'Or maybe mix in with this lot coming along behind us.'

I heard the blast of a whistle, and the rattle of a gangplank being hauled in. Looking back, I saw the traders moving away from the ship's side, pushing their handcarts.

'The guards'll be used to them,' Joe said. 'If we mix in we should be able to slip through. Act natural, and don't look their way.'

As the traders came up, we went along with them. They were talking among themselves, and ignored us. I did my best to do the same with the guards but it wasn't easy, especially when, out of the corner of my eye, I saw one start to unsling his gun. But he only rubbed his shoulder and slung it on the other side.

Joe said, in a low voice: 'Nearly there. Steady as you go.'

Then the barrier was behind us and we had reached the end of the quay. Immediately in front a man pushed a cart loaded with pots, while his wife talked about buying fish for supper. A market was spread out along the front, the nearest stall heaped with shellfish: yellow whelks, white cockles, bright red crabs and lobsters.

'Better walk on a bit,' Joe said. 'After that we'll see about getting our bearings.'

The man's hand was on Joe's shoulder before I noticed him. He was tall and black-moustached, dressed in a brown tunic and trousers. The tunic had epaulettes, and he wore a peaked cap. Automatically Joe shrugged off the hand and the two stared at one another. The man's nose was sharp, between grey sunken eyes. In a bleak voice, he said:

'You wouldn't be thinking of giving trouble, would you?'

I saw Joe's right hand clench, but he said nothing. A second man came in from the other side.

'Right then,' the first said. 'Come along, the three of you.'

The building to which we were taken overlooked the harbour. From the window I could see the cargo ship heading for the open sea. It looked a good place to be. The room we were in was small, with gloomy green walls marked by damp stains, a ceiling that had darkened to grubby yellow and a planked floor. There was a smell of dust and ink.

The man who had put his hand on Joe's shoulder sat behind a desk, looking through documents. Joe stood between Paddy and me, an arm behind each of us. Silence, broken only by the rustle of paper, pressed heavier as time crawled by. After interminable minutes the door opened and the second man appeared, accompanied by the soldiers from the quay. They still had their guns, and for a pulse-chilling moment I wondered if this could be an execution squad.

The man behind the desk barked an order and they faced him at attention, thumbs pointing rigidly along the seams of their trousers. I noticed something which first relieved me, then alarmed me further: the hand of the soldier nearer to me was trembling.

'Troopers Growcott and Benton, Second Platoon, C company, Colonel Markham's brigade – correct?'

The soldier on the right braced himself. 'Yes, sir!'

'Assigned to harbour duty, such duty to include checking all strangers seeking to enter the General's territory. About turn!' They spun round, with a clomp of feet. 'See these three?'

The one with the trembling hand didn't look much older than I was. His face was round and red, and he swallowed hard.

'These foreigners,' the man with the peaked cap said, 'entered General Pengelly's territory during your period of duty, without challenge. Do you offer any excuse?'

'The traders were coming off. We didn't see . . .'

'No.' The voice was indifferent. 'You didn't see them. Perhaps your company commander will give you reason to be more observant. You are on report. Dismiss.'

They were marched out, a look of plain fear on the younger soldier's face, and he turned to us. 'Names.'

'Joe Hardwick. And this is . . .'

'They can speak for themselves.' His finger pointed. 'You.'

'Patricia Ryan.'

'And you, boy?'

'Ben,' I said.

'Ben what?'

It had always been simply Ben. At school I had been called Ben Ryan. I had known it was wrong – assumed I was an orphan – but had left it at that. Ben son–of–the–Master? I said

46

'Just Ben, sir.'

He shook his head impatiently, but returned to Joe. 'Place of origin?'

'The Western Isles.'

'All three of you?'

'Yes.'

He tapped a pencil on his desk, stretched back in his chair; then got up and left the room. A key turned in the lock behind him.

At least we were on our own, and could talk. I asked Joe: 'What's going to happen?'

'Nothing much, I'd think. They may say we've got to go back. And as to that, once we're at sea we can go wherever we choose.'

'Those soldiers . . .'

'What of 'em?'

'He said they were on report. Does that mean they'll be punished, for letting us through?'

'Maybe so.'

'What will they do to them?'

'I don't know, never having been a soldier nor wanted to be. Give 'em extra duties, perhaps.'

I did not believe it was a prospect of extra duties that had made the young soldier tremble, and didn't think Joe did either. And if their own men were so fearful, what might happen to those responsible for getting them into trouble?

Paddy said: 'Do you think there's any chance of getting out of the window?'

We went to look. The window was sealed shut, and breaking it wouldn't help. The building was as tall as Demons' laws allowed: we were directly under the roof and the roof was an overhang.

Gazing at the harbour, Joe said: 'The soldiers let us

through. The lot who picked us up must be police. But how did they come to be looking out for us? That's the funny part.'

Soldiers and police were mainland words. I was beginning to realize how different things might be here.

Joe went on: 'One thing: it's the soldiers that have guns. The others don't, far as I can see. If he comes back on his own, I reckon I can handle him. It's worth a try. When I do, you two get going quick.'

'We'll tackle him with you,' Paddy said.

'You'd only get in the way. Do as I say.'

Paddy caught my eye behind his back, and I nodded agreement. But even if we overpowered the policeman without him managing to call for help, we still had to get clear of the building. I'd seen three or four policemen downstairs as we were brought in, but there were probably more. We would really be in trouble then.

Time dragged again. The window faced south, and a sun slowly sinking against a screen of unbroken blue. The room was airless and stuffy. Occasionally we heard footsteps, but they did not stop.

Finally some did. A key turned, and the door started to open.

'Let him get inside,' Joe whispered. 'And leave it to me!'

The policeman in the peaked cap appeared, to my surprise, with a smile of a sort on his face. But that was nothing to my amazement at seeing the person who followed him. I ran towards Mother Ryan, but Paddy got there first.

The following morning Paddy and I sat under an oak tree at the top of a sloping meadow. Below us, a long way off, a narrow band of blue marked the sea. Higher up, surrounded by ornamental gardens on several levels, stood the villa of General Pengelly.

It was very big, with four wings branching out from a central courtyard where water gushed from the mouth of a huge bronze fish into a marble pool swarming with real fish, crimson and black and yellow. The air thereabouts was full of song from birds in painted wicker cages, suspended from poles set among large red pots filled with glossy green plants.

In the room I had been given, the walls and even the bed were decorated with flowers. There were bright rugs on the floor, and a marble-topped wash-stand to which a serving girl had brought me a pitcher of hot water for washing. There were servants everywhere inside the house, and at least half a dozen men looking after the gardens.

Dinner had offered another taste of luxury. The most prominent item was a vast salmon on a long silver dish, but there had also been joints of beef, ham, pork and venison, and a selection of side dishes offering treats I had never seen before. There had been a tempting array of puddings too: I sampled three before reaching saturation point.

I said to Paddy: 'It's a bit different from what we expected.'

'What did you expect?'

'Well, nothing like this. Did you?'

After a pause, Paddy said: 'I'd like to know why.'

'Why what?'

'Why bring us here?'

'Because Mother asked, of course, after the police made their report to the General.'

'But why were she and Antonia here, in the first place?'

'Perhaps he was sorry for them being sent away from the Isles. They seem nice people.'

'You didn't think so yesterday.'

'That was a mistake. They didn't know who we were.'

'I asked Ralph about the soldiers: would they still get into trouble for letting us through? And what would happen to them.'

'What did he say?'

'He said he didn't know. And he made a joke about the soldiers needing glasses if they couldn't spot an islander. He wanted to change the subject.'

'I like Ralph,' I said.

He was about twenty, tall and dark and athletic. He seemed to smile more than most of the people here, though as the General's only son he probably had more to smile about.

'So does Antonia.'

'Don't you?'

'He's probably all right.' She paused again. 'I'd just like to know *why* we're being so well treated.'

'Does it matter?'

She did not answer, and I let it go. A lot had happened in the past week, nearly all unpleasant. I couldn't see the point in worrying about something pleasant. I lay back, closing my eyes, opening them when Paddy cried:

'Joe!'

He came lumbering down the slope. 'Mother Ryan said I'd find you somewhere round here, to bid farewell.'

'You're not going?' Paddy said.

'Have to. Things need seeing to on the island.'

I said: 'There's no hurry. Andy's there.'

Joe laughed. 'And that's a good reason for getting back!'

Paddy said: 'By now Sheriff Wilson will know you helped us get away.'

'He might guess it.'

'You could get into trouble.'

'Guessing's one thing, proving's another. No one ever knows where my boat is or has been, and not even the

Sheriff will lay charges against a fisherman without solid evidence. I've good mates. I'll be all right; as well off there as here, certain sure.'

'It's better than you said,' I told him.

'You reckon?'

'They served a salmon at dinner last night which must have weighed fifteen kilos. I reckon whoever landed it had a fight on his hands.'

Joe shook his head. 'It didn't come out of the sea.'

'Sea or river, it would have taken some holding.'

'They grow 'em from fry, in reservoirs. One of the men was telling me.'

His voice was scornful. I said: 'There's so much here, of everything.'

'For some. I had my supper with the servants, and we didn't have those sort of victuals. I'd better be on my way.'

'I wish I was coming with you,' Paddy said.

She would say that. 'You'll be all right,' Joe said. He gave her a hug, and he and I shook hands. 'Maybe things will sort themselves out, and you'll all come back and we'll build a new house on Old Isle.' He grinned at me. 'For the new Master.'

Paddy said: 'You'll look after Liza and the kittens?'

'I will. Though cats can look after themselves. Better than people mostly.'

General Pengelly was tall and grey-bearded, thin but pot-bellied, and I hardly ever saw him without a pipe in his mouth, even at the dinner table. The smell was sweetish and not unpleasant, but it permeated everything. He had a soft slow voice you had to strain to hear.

Apart from Ralph, he had a wife and two daughters. Rachel and Millicent were in their middle twenties: one tall, one short and plump, both plain. The wife's name was

Maud, but everyone including the General addressed her as Mistress. She too was tall, and one could see that, unlike her daughters, she had been handsome. But her expression was grim, her infrequent smile stiff.

Everyone here wore sombre clothes. The ladies' every-day dresses were dark grey, though that of the Mistress had a white collar. Mother Ryan and Antonia had been given similar dresses, and Paddy one that had probably originated with Millicent: the length was about right but it was much too full.

The General presided over the dining table from a broad chair with wide flat arms. His wife kept a close scrutiny on the company from the far end, maintaining a generally forbidding attitude to all except her son. Him she fussed, selecting titbits for his plate. I saw him smile and shrug at Antonia while she was doing this.

Strict rules of discipline were enforced in the household. Servants had to bow or curtsy at each encounter with a member of the family (which for the moment appeared to include us), and were lined up at nine each morning for inspection by the Mistress. There were rules for children too. Paddy and I were told we must never speak to an adult without being spoken to, must never run or even walk quickly inside the house, and must respond to the first gong for meals and be present, at attention behind our chairs, by the time the second gong summoned the others.

But obeying the rules was all that was required. No one said anything about school, and we didn't ask. We found our way to the sea on the third morning. The beach was coarse shingle, unlike the fine yellow sand we were used to, but we could swim and there were caves and rock pools to explore.

As she poked a crab into activity, Paddy said: 'I've found out why we're here. And why we're being so well treated.'

'Go on.'

'You know Ralph's an officer in the police? He was on duty the day Mother and Antonia were landed from the *Hesperus*.'

'Well?'

'One of the other officers was going to send them to some sort of prison, until they could be sent on to Ireland. When he saw them, Ralph had them brought here instead.' When I looked blank, she added: 'Because of Antonia.'

'Antonia?'

'Because he's keen on her, fool. Like Bob Marriton, who came courting from January Island.'

I said: 'I see,' but didn't properly. 'Do you think she's keen on him?'

'I don't know.' She looked down at her dress in disgust. 'Dark clothes are all right for her – with blonde hair. And hers fit her. This is *awful*.'

It didn't look particularly awful to me, but I thought it better to say nothing. The crab stopped pretending to be dead, and darted away and was lost in weed.

'Anyway,' Paddy said, 'that's why we're here.'

5

On our first Sunday in the villa I awoke to wind blustering against my open window and chill rain in my face when I got out of bed to close it. A few hardy birds were singing, but the sky was dark. When the stable clock chimed three quarters, I was not sure if it heralded seven or eight. In either case it would have been too late to go back to bed, so I washed and dressed and headed for the dining room.

Despite the unpromising morning, or maybe because of it, I was keenly looking forward to breakfast. This was the one meal which involved no formality: one helped oneself from candle-warmed dishes laid out on the long oak sideboard. These would be appetizingly piled with bacon and grilled ham, sausages, kidneys, black pudding, golden potatoes, fried and scrambled eggs.

I was aware of missing the pungent scents of bacon and coffee before I entered. When I did, I found the sideboard offering nothing but baskets of bread and jugs of water. I was trying to work out what was wrong when Ralph came in.

'Ben! I'm glad to see you're an early Sunday riser. I doubt if we'll see my sisters before noon, if then.' He put bread on a plate and filled a glass. 'Not eating?' He noticed my expression. 'Of course, it's your first fast day. Tony found it a shock, too.'

He meant Antonia I realized, with some surprise. As I

unenthusiastically took a couple of chunks of bread, he went on:

'I hadn't realized you weren't taught to fast all day before a Summoning, in those islands of yours. I should imagine there's quite a bit you'll need to learn, one way and another.'

I wondered if Antonia had told him that in fact we didn't have Summonings on Old Isle. And even on Sheriff's, no special preparations were involved, and no fasting: the Sunday midday meal was the main one of the week. There might indeed be things to learn – for instance, how to get by on bread and water for the next several hours.

When we were first brought to the villa, I had noticed an old mill, standing in flat uncultivated ground between two forks of road and seeming utterly deserted, though a broad well-trodden path led towards it. Unattractive in afternoon sunshine, it looked positively ugly in the twilight of a day during which the sun had never succeeded in penetrating heavy clouds that raced in on a harrying wind.

We had all, including the General, walked the distance of perhaps a thousand metres from the villa. Others must have travelled much further on foot, from the town and still more outlying parts. There were hundreds, all dressed in black – I had been provided with a black smock reaching almost to my ankles. They crowded together on the rain-sodden ground in front of the mill, but left a path for the General's party, and the Summoner who accompanied us. As we passed I saw their faces: there was grimness and apprehension in them, but expectancy too.

The nearer we got the more plainly ruinous the mill was shown to be. It could not have been put to its proper purpose for many years. It was just a black and broken tower: even under this darkening sky I was able to see through a gaping window to a hole in the further wall. I thought of Paddy's remark on John's Isle, about Demons perching on a windmill's sails. They could scarcely do so here, where even the frame had long since rotted away.

Standing on a stone slab in front of the ragged hole which had been the mill's front door, the Summoner bowed ceremoniously to General Pengelly, who bowed stiffly in return. He was physically almost an opposite to Summoner Hawkins, being squat and amply fleshed. But as he launched into his address, his tone was no less threatening.

It was as sinners, he told us, that we were assembled: wretched guilty worthless sinners. There was none present who had not in some way offended against the Dark One. Most of us were deeply sunk in iniquity, many lost to salvation and hope. Day by day we committed wickedness, breaking the laws laid down to guide us.

Those laws were plain enough. There must be no truck with machines, which in the past had led men to perdition, and no voyaging far from shore, into seas where the Madness lingered. Apart from that, there was the simple duty of obedience. The child must obey its parents, servants their masters, soldiers their General. And this obedience was part of a greater serving – of the dread ruler of the universe, the Dark One. The laws were not difficult to understand, yet men and women and children continually transgressed against them.

'But', he cried, 'the Dark One is not mocked! His purposes cannot be frustrated by puny mortals. Rebellion will earn undying torment, obedience the blissful reward of being given wings to fly above the dark Moon-valleys, and watch the damned as they writhe in hell-fire.'

His voice pierced through a gusting wind. 'The fool in his folly declares himself contented with the day. He has eaten and drunk, his house is roofed and his hearth warmed. He has a wife to his bed, children to bear his name.'

The Summoner paused, but, resuming, lifted his voice to a shout. 'So much for the day — but look what follows! There will come a dusk of Demons, to seek out the fool and pluck him from wife and child, from home and hearth, to lift him high and carry him far, and pitch him at last into the unquenchable flames . . .

'Abase yourselves therefore: abase yourselves and repent your follies. Kneel before the Dark One, and the Demons that do his will . . .'

Beside the Summoner the General dropped clumsily to his knees, and the rest of the congregation followed suit. I felt the chill of wet earth on my knees through the thin smock. Some, I saw, had prostrated themselves completely.

'Repent,' the Summoner shouted. 'Repent, and beg mercy of the Dark One!'

He had repeated that cry four or five times before the darkness overhead started to lighten. I looked up and saw brightness spreading out from the broken top of the mill. It was something like moonlight, but more intense and more beautiful. At the centre of the brilliance I noticed a single spot of black; but that spot grew, and grew.

They came out of that, swelling until they appeared to fill the sky. I saw a writhing tangle of shapes, winged and scaled and slimy, rotting faces oozing filth, hideous reptilian arms stretching out . . . reaching down to grasp me. All round I heard shrieks of fear, cries for mercy.

The Demons were crying now too, a stridulation that rose above that clamour and seemed to pierce the skull. They used no words I could understand, but their hatred was plain and so was the message they conveyed: there could be no hope of resisting their anger, no end for their victims but a hideous death and after that damnation.

The phantoms in my nightmare had been terrifying, but one woke from dreams. This time I knew I was not sleeping. The horror was real, and inescapable.

Terror distorted time. I could not tell how long it lasted, but eventually an end did come. The Demons faded from the sky, the Summoner spoke a final prayer to the Dark One, and we scrambled awkwardly to our feet. Slowly the congregation dispersed; first in silence, then whispering, at last openly chattering. From relief, I guessed, but not merely from relief. I detected excitement in their voices, like magpies round a carcase. I did not care for that sound, either.

The following day was market day, and just after ten o'clock a small procession set off from the villa, headed by the General's carriage. This was an opulent vehicle, drawn by two handsome black horses with plumed headbands, which had cushioned seats and windows for protection against bad weather. The Mistress and her daughters rode in that, wearing dark grey cloaks over their dark grey dresses but with hats sporting little coloured feathers for the occasion. The General and Ralph had, as usual, ridden down to the town immediately after breakfast.

Mother Ryan, Antonia, Paddy and I followed in an open trap drawn by an old chestnut cob. A clattering wagon, pulled by an even greater dobbin of a horse with a wall eye and crammed with servants who had been given brief leave from their duties, brought up the rear of the cavalcade.

The carriage wheels scattered spray which occasionally blew back into our faces; but the sun came out as we set off. There was woodland immediately below the villa, but the road soon emerged into fields. That was where it forked, one heavily potholed branch heading north, the other curving round the hill towards the town. I looked towards the mill as we passed it. There was no appearance of menace now, but I shuddered at the sight of it.

We were quickly past though, and into the outskirts of the town. Not long after, our convoy came to a halt in the main square, and Paddy and I hastened to scramble down from the trap. We were eager to explore the market, and the Mistress had promised us money to spend.

The square was dominated by a red brick building, fronted by a white-columned portico, which was the Court House, the seat of General Pengelly's authority. The big carriage had drawn up directly outside, and a uniformed servant was helping the Mistress to alight. I headed that way, but stopped as I heard Paddy's voice raised behind me. I thought she might be rebuking my haste to get the spending money; but when I turned, embarrassed, she was not looking my way. I followed her gaze, and saw him standing, white-shirted among the press of grey, his black beard unmistakable.

'Joe!' I called. We raced to reach him and confused him with questions.

'Easy,' he said. 'Easy. One of you at a time.'

'Has the Sheriff banished you too?' Paddy asked. 'Are you in trouble because of us?'

'Mother Ryan will get the General to help you,' I said.

I looked for her, but Joe shook his head. 'No trouble. All's well. I brought Sheriff Wilson across this morning, and he paid me for it. Paid me well. He's not usually so generous.'

'The Sheriff?' I said, and was alarmed. The days of imprisonment and isolation, of sitting opposite him at table in an atmosphere of silent menace, came sharply back. 'Here – on the mainland?'

'Nay, more than that. Here, in this Court House place.

Along with the General. And it's you they want to see, young Ben, both on 'em. I was told you'd be coming down with the main party and put to watch for you.'

My alarm was heightened by a sense of being trapped. Both of them? Joe said:

'I went back to the isle first, to see to things. When I next landed on Sheriff's, his men were waiting on the quay. He didn't ask where I'd been or what I'd been about.' Joe shook his head. 'He knew just where you were and told me he wanted taking there. I had my doubts at first, but he swore no harm was intended ye. Swore it on the Dark One. He were altogether pleasant, which surprised me somewhat. But how did he know – where you were, I mean? That's the puzzle of it. Anyway, I can vouch he's in a better temper. You'd better do as he wants and go on inside and see him, all the same. Important men don't care to be kept waiting, and it don't cost much to humour them. Paddy'll keep me company while ye're about whatever ye're about.'

The General was wearing his uniform: royal blue with gold buttons, a high silver collar and silver markings on the sleeves. Sheriff Wilson had a dark blue shirt and trousers under his crimson cloak. I felt drab and insignificant in my shapeless grey tunic.

Despite Joe's reassurance, my apprehension increased as the guard ushered me into the General's office. It was a big room, with a floor of alternating black and white squares of polished stone on which footsteps echoed disconcertingly, and a long table set out with miniature figures of soldiers in a scene of battle. There was also a large desk, behind which sat the General in a leather armchair which he swivelled to look at me. On the other side, the Sheriff was in a smaller chair that did not swivel, so he had to turn his head. The affable smile was back on his face. I knew better than to trust it, but even an untrustworthy smile was more reassuring than a frown.

The General was smiling too. I advanced warily, bowing to him first. He said, in his soft faint voice:

'Sheriff Wilson has something to tell you, Ben.'

He indicated an empty chair next to the Sheriff's. I said:

'I'll stand, sir, thank you.'

'It's good to see you again, Ben,' the Sheriff said, and nodded amiably. 'I can see you are being well looked after. But I'm sure you will be glad to be back in your homeland.' I looked at him in disbelief, and he went on: 'There has been an unhappy misunderstanding. It appears Summoner Hawkins misinterpreted the intention of the Demons.'

A joke, I wondered? But although a smiling he was scarcely a joking man. He said:

'The Demons did not burn your father's house in anger. It was done rather as a mark of respect to one who had been a faithful servant of the Dark One. The house was sacred to his memory, not to be used or dwelt in by any other. It is more proper to build a new house for the new Master – for you, Ben.'

I stared in utter incredulity.

'We have already put workmen to clearing the rubble. A house will be built on Old Isle to your directions. Meanwhile, you will be given accommodation on Sheriff's that befits your status.'

It had to be a trick. The General, though, had taken us in when we were fugitives. I appealed to him.

'Do I have to go back?'

'No, Ben,' he said. He glanced at the Sheriff, with a look of satisfaction. It was almost as though they were competing for an important possession, but that was absurd. 'You are at liberty to stay here, if you wish. The choice is yours.'

Before I could speak, the Sheriff said: 'You may, of course, bring Mrs Ryan and her daughters back with you. That was another misunderstanding. You can bring whomever you wish to the Isles. They will be most welcome, and I am sure you will want them with you when your new house is built.'

'If that is what you choose,' the General said.

It was him again I looked to. 'Do I have to decide right away?'

They both said 'No', but the General seemed the more pleased of the two. My head was spinning, and I wanted to get out of the room and talk to Paddy. I said:

'I'll think about it, sir. May I go now?'

The General nodded affably. As I turned away, the Sheriff stood up and started towards me. Involuntarily I drew back, but he only pointed to my neck.

'What's that, Ben?'

'What, sir?'

He put out a hand to the chain which must have been visible inside my open shirt. He drew out the medallion, and examined it.

'Who gave you this? Your father?'

'Mother Ryan gave it to me, but it was from him. She said he always wore it.'

He dropped it back, his fingers unpleasantly warm against my skin. 'And so you must, Ben. It is the symbol of your inheritance. Keep it with you, always.'

'Yes, sir. May I go now?'

The Sheriff nodded. 'Go, Ben, and think about it. To be Master of Old Isle, as your father was before you . . . But meanwhile we know you are safe and know where you are.' He smiled, and I wondered again that an expression normally registering amiability could seem so malign. 'We found you here, and will always find you, wherever you may be. Remember that.'

★

While I had been in the General's office, Mrs Pengelly had given money to Paddy: a whole shilling for each of us. We were free, she had said, to explore the market until three o'clock, and had told Paddy there was no excuse for being late for the return journey because the Court House clock chimed both hours and quarters.

My impulse had been to blurt out my news, but I did not. At first that was because of Joe: he would, I knew, be delighted at the prospect of all of us returning to the Isles, and hurt if I showed hesitance. When Paddy asked what they had wanted with me, I said nothing much and suggested Joe might explore the market with us. He shook his big head emphatically: he could not be doing for long with mainlanders and their ways. He was glad to have seen us, and hoped he soon would again, but his boat waited in the harbour and the return journey to the Isles, against the prevailing wind, would not be easy.

As we watched him stride away, I reflected that mine should not have been a difficult decision. Joe was returning to the place I knew and loved. It would be good to be with him there, still better to be the means of taking back Mother Ryan and Antonia and Paddy. Even if I did not trust the Sheriff, what could he do to harm us? The Demons had spoken, and I was confirmed as Master of Old Isle. And there was to be a new house built for us, to my specifications!

Although I was free now to speak of it to Paddy, I found myself strangely reluctant. For one thing, I realized that talking about the restoration of my status as Master might well invite her ridicule. And my own feelings about what had happened were confused. It had been so unexpected, and much of it was still puzzling. I felt I needed to think about it before I spoke to anyone. Meanwhile, the market lay before us. I put consideration of the future to one side, and we pushed through the press of people, hand in hand.

Between the main square and the sea front, stalls had been set up in almost every street and alleyway. Country people had brought in all manner of goods: meat, cheeses, vegetables, fresh-water fish, dried apples and tomatoes, pickled eggs, pies and cakes and biscuits. There were stalls selling shirts, frocks, knitted stockings, pots and plates and cutlery of both wood and iron. What had taken place in the General's office may have been very important, but my immediate interest was engaged here. One stall was given over to wooden clocks with pendulum weights and painted faces, some with little panels that opened on the hour to release a calling bird. Eleven was striking, and the air was loud with hoots and trills and cuckooings. I was fascinated but Paddy dragged me away, pointing out that our two shillings would not run to even the smallest of them.

Instead, for a couple of pennies, we took the edge off our hunger with lardy cake and lemonade at a nearby stall, and roamed on. There was so much more to see within a few metres than in the whole of Sheriff's. I privately vowed I would re-visit the market after we were back on Old Isle: Joe would bring us across. I could not resist a thrill of satisfaction in thinking I would have the power to do that, and other things as well.

Among a heap of junk I discovered an ancient knife which had not merely blades but a little·saw, a file, a fish scaler and a corkscrew – and a tiny pair of folding scissors! Six precious pence went on that, but I could not imagine money better spent. At the same stall, for tuppence, Paddy got a glass pendant showing a white eye against a turquoise background. An amulet against Demons, the store-holder said, but she said she bought it simply because she liked it.

Time, which recently had often crawled, now galloped.

The Court House clock struck twice, and then chimed a first quarter. We had reached a square with entertainments on offer, and watched the end of a Punch-and-Judy show. A tent nearby bore a sign:

FANTASTIC CREATURES.

Underneath, straggling writing proclaimed:

See the Mermaid, Queen of the Watery Deep!
See the Giant Tortoise, a Thousand Years Old!
See the Bear that Walks like a Man!
See the Monkey . . . Giant Rat . . . Talking Bird!

The notion of being within reach of such wonders and not viewing them was unthinkable; but another sign read 'Admission Two Pence', and my purchase of the knife had emptied my pocket. It was lucky Paddy had enough left to pay for us both.

The money was taken by an old fat woman sitting beneath the sign, who wheezed like a broken-winded horse as she opened the tent flap to admit us to a scene of dimness and unsettling scents. The only light came from a flickering oil-lamp tied to a tent pole. The smells were rank: they sickened me a little but were exciting too.

Sounds were disturbing also. A hairy, brown creature, no bigger than a baby and somewhat similar except for having a flat wrinkled face, showed yellow teeth as it chattered angrily. And that noise was pierced by screams from the shiny, curving beak of a big bird, feathered part green, part red, which hopped from foot to foot on a perch within a wooden hoop. The monkey, and the talking bird . . . in the background shadows a large mound that heaved and snored must be the bear.

A man, old like the woman but small and wiry, sat in a battered armchair. He had a ragged white beard, specked with black, and one eye closed and sunken. In an outlandish accent, he growled:

'Young sir – mam'selle – welcome! Do not fear these remarkable beasts, but neither venture too close. Poll there may draw blood from an impertinent finger. That apart, look freely – feast your eyes. These are marvels such as you will not soon see again.'

In disappointing fact, there was not all that much to see. The mermaid, a fish-like thing with a face resembling the monkey's, was stuffed; and there was nothing to the giant tortoise but an empty shell, though admittedly that was over a metre long. True, the giant rat was alive. It crouched in a wire cage, eating roots and snuffling, ten times as big as any rat I'd seen; but it lacked a tail and looked more like an oversized guinea-pig.

There were other disillusionments. The monkey was bald in patches and mange-ridden. Paddy asked to hear the bird talk: after much chivvying and prompting from the old man, it squawked 'Pretty Polly' and relapsed into screams and silence.

The man, on the other hand, turned garrulous, telling of his adventures in accumulating the items on display. He spoke of ice mountains floating in the sea, sands too hot to tread, prodigious steamy forests where monkeys leapt from branch to branch while snakes of enormous length writhed and hissed and flashed forked tongues beneath. He swore if he talked till nightfall, he could not begin to convey the wonders of the lands he had visited.

He talked too much, and I sensed scepticism in Paddy; but I could not help being excited by his stories. They struck that chord in me which had been touched by the pictures in the book we found in the ruins on Sheriff's – and those other pictures of great ships, on the corridor wall in the Master's house. This was another hint of a world that might exist beyond the world of ordinary living – no, not just a hint, a promise almost. There was, I was sure, more to life than so far had appeared: much more.

The old man fixed his single eye on me. 'And yet you, I would hazard, are a likely lad for adventuring. Most landsmen are dogs, ready to snarl or wag tail as their masters bid them. You have the look of a boy of spirit.'

The flattery, I guessed, like the talk, was meant to compensate for the inadequacy of his show: he had already told Paddy that though he had met with comely maidens in a score of countries he had seen few as pretty – nay, none! It had its effect, all the same. I told him I was not locally born, but from the Western Isles. He nodded, and winked the single eye.

'Did I not judge you soundly? A man of the sea, as I am! Born to wind and spray, and a sky untroubled by Demons. Lad, you must not rot away in this dull clime, but seek marvels while the spring is in your limbs. Would I enjoyed your green youth still!'

Even though I knew it for flattery, I was affected by it; and intrigued by the thought of travelling to strange lands. That too was surely something a Master of Old Isle could do, if he chose. My father had never left the island, but he had been an old man. In his younger days there had obviously been journeyings. I too might explore the world – perhaps even discover the mysterious land from which he had come.

Paddy, though, was plainly bored. She had not warmed to his remark about comely maidens, and cared even less for the urgings that were addressed to me. The old man did his best to keep us, making a fresh but unsuccessful attempt to provoke the bird to talk, prodding the giant rat to abandon its gnawing at roots and run laboriously about the cage, finally waking the bear to tower sleepily over us.

It yawned bad breath, and Paddy said firmly that we must leave. He was rambling about moonlit tropic seas as we scrambled into the sweeter-smelling air.

And into the arms, almost, of General Pengelly. Paddy, in her haste to be away, did not look where she was going, and his hand caught and steadied her. He frowned towards the tent.

'You keep poor company.' The fat woman bowed and gabbled respects. 'You should have no truck with such people – as well go vagabonding with gypsies.' The clock struck its third quarter. 'And anyway it is time you were back.'

He accompanied us to the square, lecturing us – though not unkindly. While it was the people of the tent who had provoked his disapproval, his condemnations ranged wider. We were from a far-away place, an island – he spoke the word with distaste – and had lacked proper instruction. We must understand there were two sorts of human kind: landsmen and sea-people. The former were honest, respectable, worthy; the latter shiftless, dissembling, treacherous. The Madness had begun in them, and likely lingered still. A sensible boy – or girl, nodding at Paddy – kept clear of such.

Advice, he continued, addressing me, was a coin a wise man expended prudently. It was likely to be wasted on many, but capable of good return among the deserving few. He had studied me and saw me as promising, worthy of the trouble he was taking.

I was not so much impressed by the advice as by the fact of its bestowal. In my growing up I had been surrounded by feminine company and known little of masculine approval. The Master had ignored me, and Andy only noticed me to mock. Joe had provided more, but made no secret of his greater fondness for Paddy. Now, within a space of minutes, two men had paid me attention, one calling me a likely lad, the other promising. Being accepted as a successor to the Master was heady stuff: this was more down to earth, more believable and in an odd way more satisfying.

Back at the villa, Paddy was out of sorts. When I spoke of the creatures in the tent, she snapped that they were a ridiculous cheat – either dead or sick, in any case stinking. The mermaid, she would swear, was monkey sewn on to fish. When, for the sake of peace, I agreed, and mentioned the General's condemnation of the show-people, she was not mollified: he was no better, a narrow-minded old fool, as nasty as the rest of them here.

At that, I remonstrated. We were being well looked after, better than we had any reason to expect. No one could call Ralph nasty. The Mistress had given us the money to spend in the market, and the General too seemed kindly.

'Because he called you promising!' she said scornfully. 'It doesn't take much to win you. I hate it here.'

It was not often that I had an opportunity to impress her, and I could not resist seizing it. I said:

'I can take you back to Old Isle, if you want – take all of us.'

Paddy laughed. 'You're mad! Have you forgotten Joe and I had to help you get away?' She stopped, and looked at me suspiciously. 'The Sheriff and General Pengelly – just what *did* happen when they saw you this morning?'

I told her then, as simply as I could. She said:

'But why? It makes no sense.'

I shrugged. 'It's what the Demons say.'

'Then if you're not mad, they must be.' We were in the garden, and she saw me glance involuntarily towards the sky where a pale moon was beginning to turn silver in the dusk. 'Oh, don't be silly. Even if they could, they're not likely to waste time spying on people like us. What are you going to do?'

I knew what she meant, but hedged. 'About what?'

'Staying or going back,' she said impatiently.

'I told them I'd think about it. But if you want to go back . . .'

'It's nothing to do with me. You're the one they're going to build a house for.'

'You did say you hated it here.'

'Doesn't mean I want to go back *there*. Not after the way Sheriff Wilson treated us.' There was frost in her voice. 'Maybe it's different for you, being the new Master.'

I looked at her helplessly. I knew nothing was simple, but was learning there are always more complications than you imagine. Perhaps Mother Ryan could help me: she always had done.

6

I did not see Mother Ryan that evening. She and Antonia were at a musical entertainment, presided over by the Mistress, which followed market day and lasted beyond the bed-time imposed for children. In the morning though, I sought her out in her room.

She listened while I told her what the Sheriff and General Pengelly had said, and was silent after I had finished. Her silence confirmed the truth of what I still found difficulty in believing. I said: 'What do you think we should do, Mother?'

She said slowly: 'I think you should go back, Ben. It's your inheritance.'

'And you'll come too?'

She paused. 'One day, maybe.' She saw my face. 'It's not easy.'

'But why *not*? Paddy said she didn't want to because of what happened – the Sheriff sending you away and shutting me up. But that's all changed. He has to obey the Demons, and the Demons have said I'm to be Master. We don't even need to see the Sheriff once we're back on Old Isle.'

She was sitting in an armchair, and I had been addressing her from a long-familiar position, curled up against her knee. She put her hand on my head, stroking.

'If it was just the two of us . . .'

'Paddy . . .'

71

'Ah, don't mind Paddy. Whatever she says in her moods, she'd follow you anywhere, any time. But I've Antonia to think of.'

'I've said: Antonia can come as well. Anyone I say can come.'

'I'm sure 'tis so. And no more than your due, being son of the Master.' She sighed. 'But even such a one cannot tell a young girl what's right for her.'

'You mean, because of her and Ralph? But he can visit; and she could visit him.' I thought of the long stretch of heaving waters between the Western Isles and the mainland. 'In summer, it's not too bad a journey.'

She caught a lock of my hair and tugged it. 'When I was your age, my mother used to say "You'll understand better when you grow up". I hated that, but it's often true. The importance of things changes. The way it is just now I'd never get her away from here even for a week, and if I did there'd be nothing but moping and melancholy.'

I shook my head. 'I don't understand.'

Mother Ryan laughed. 'Didn't I say as much!'

'But if you're not going back, neither am I. I'll tell the General so.'

'I suppose it's you must decide. And your inheritance won't be lost for your being a while on the mainland.' She rose from the chair, and I too got to my feet. 'Things may alter. In time, they always do. I don't think I could go on too long like this, with no occupation and people fetching and carrying for me. I've been used to working all my life, but never dreamed how much I'd come to miss it.'

That at least I understood. Unlimited leisure – no coal to bring in, logs to saw, horses to muck out – had seemed a very fair compensation for having to obey petty rules; but already it had begun to pall. Coming from her room, I saw a lad not much older than myself drawing water from the well at the rear of the villa, and offered him a hand. He shook his head dumbly, looking surprised.

Antonia found me wandering in the flower gardens.

'Nothing to do, Ben? Then we're in the same boat. The Mistress has her dressmaker in this morning, so our company is not required. Paddy in the sulks?'

I was never sure of Antonia's own mood. I said warily: 'Sort of.'

'Poor Ben.'

She was wearing a broad-rimmed hat which hid her face, but I assumed she was being sarcastic, as usual. I moved away, but she followed me.

'Do you like it here?'

I didn't see how I could discuss the latest turn of events with her, after what Mother Ryan had said, though I supposed she might have heard something from Ralph. I said:

'It's all right.'

'Do you like the General?'

'I suppose so.' I thought about it. 'Yes, I do.'

'I do, too. He has that quiet way of speaking, but he's strong, and protective. Like the Master.'

I was startled. 'The Master? Protective?'

'The way he used to be, in Ireland. I remember it from when I was little. He used to throw me up in the air, and I loved it, knowing he was there to catch me. He was always laughing in those days.'

'He changed a lot then.'

'People do. Some people, anyway.'

We had reached an arbour, covered with forsythia in full bloom. She leaned against a wall of bright yellow, tilting her face to the sun. She looked relaxed and happy, and I realized with surprise that in her thin pale way she was quite pretty.

'How about Ralph?' she asked abruptly. 'Do you like him?'

I said 'Yes' immediately, and with conviction.

After a pause, she said: 'It's good here.' She was smiling, her eyes closed against the sunshine. 'I don't think I'd mind if I never lived anywhere else.'

So that, I thought, was that. I could not imagine going back to the Isles on my own, Mother Ryan wouldn't go without Antonia, and Antonia wouldn't leave Ralph. I was not greatly disappointed. I much preferred General Pengelly to the Sheriff, and having too little to do was a trivial complaint. Ralph would probably help me find something. The inheritance could wait. Without Mother Ryan and Paddy, it meant nothing anyway.

There was a succession of dry grey days, with a chill breeze from the north-east that occasionally strengthened to a wind. Paddy and I made peace, but a coolness lingered. She did not speak again of returning to the Western Isles, and neither did I. I might have been more bothered by her indifference if it had not been that Ralph did indeed help me fill out the idle hours. It was because of Antonia, I realized, that he had given up working in the town and stayed close to the villa, but I was glad of his company.

I went with him around the home farm, inspecting the latest farrowing of a sow, watching the smith shoe the horses, seeing how the young wheat and barley were progressing. There were also several outlying farms, managed by tenants, and one afternoon (when Ralph knew Antonia was going to be fully occupied in the women's quarters, which were forbidden to men) we rode out to one of them. He had provided me with a pony called Hussar, an easy-going roan. He was a dull beast and I thought of Black Prince, but with only a minor pang. Andy would be looking after him; he could be trusted where horses were concerned.

On the way back Ralph reined in, pointing. We were on a bridle path overlooking a sweep of valley that carried the road. A little procession of closed wagons moved slowly along it. I counted four, together with half a dozen outriders, two having laden donkeys yoked to their mounts. The wagons were painted in a variety of colours and patterns: black and white, red, yellow, green and blue. It made a pretty sight.

'Who are they?' I asked.

'Not so much who as what. They're didikoi.'

'Didi . . .?'

'Gypsies is another name. And they sometimes call themselves travellers. You'll not have seen them in your islands – nowhere to travel *to* there. They're not of our people, nor any other.'

His tone was disapproving, and I recalled the General's warning in the market. I said cautiously:

'Are they allowed to do that – travel about, and not belong?'

He shook his head. 'We wouldn't want them settled among us. They're a dirty lot. Thieves too – they'll steal livestock, money, anything they can get their hands on. Country folk are afraid of them: they think they have powers to lay spells.'

'But they don't, do they?'

'It's country talk,' he said dismissively. 'They keep their distance from *us*, and providing they do we let them be. We'd not want any kind of dealings with them. It's said the Madness runs in them still.'

From a distance the wagons looked attractive. So did the notion of travelling about the country: not confined to any one spot but finding a new scene every day. I reflected that was something I would be able to do as Master, if life on the island palled. But I had come to rely on Ralph's judgement and his hostility towards the gypsies was clearly great; and understandable if they were such thieves. And if the strange thing called the Madness lingered among them. This could be an opportunity to find out something about that.

'What was the Madness, Ralph?' I asked. 'People mention it, but no one says what it was.'

'It came of bad living. There were too many people, to start with, crowded together in towns a thousand times the size of ours. There were buildings in them more than a hundred times the height of a man. Think of it – a hundred families, one atop another, and the same next door, and tens of hundreds like that all round you.'

I asked: 'How did the ones at the top get up there? It must have taken all day, climbing the stairs.'

'They had machines for taking them up and down. There were machines for everything – for travelling faster than the wind, not only on land but through the air, for seeing and hearing what was happening on the other side of the world.'

Although the thought of people living on top of one another was unpleasant, my curiosity was sharpened by his reference to machines. Seeing and hearing things on the other side of the world – travelling through the *air* . . .? Ralph said firmly:

'It was the machines were the main trouble. They brought idleness, and idleness brought wicked living. There were no proper families, or proper rules. And what with being all crowded up, they turned on one another, fighting and killing. You get the same with hens if you pen them too close, or pigs. Children even turned on their elders, killing their grannies for pennies. That was the Madness.'

Looking over the peaceful valley, empty except for the wagons, it was hard to believe such a story, but Ralph clearly did. I asked:

'What happened then?'

'The Dark One set their machines against them. You can kill easier with machines. They died in hundreds of thousands. The ones who survived learned their lesson. They listened to the commandments of the Dark One, and went back to a wholesome way of life, with all things orderly and children obeying their parents as they ought. They learned not to go mixing themselves up but stay in their proper places, and not use the machines which had caused the mixing up. And we landsmen banned the sea-people from our shores. Sea-people are another cause of mixing. The Madness is in them still.'

'There are ships in the harbour,' I pointed out.

'From other parts of the mainland and islands close by, like those you come from. Not from the distant islands where the sea-people live. We want nothing to do with them.'

Though I was prepared to take what Ralph said on trust, questions nagged still. I said: 'We . . . I found a book once, in some ruins on Sheriff's. It had a picture of a big machine surrounded by rocks, and the words underneath were: "The first men on the Moon". You said people used to travel through the air – as far as the Moon, maybe?'

Ralph shook his head. 'Another thing they did in those days was tell lies, making up stories which weren't true. The Moon belongs to the Demons, so how could people go there unless the Demons took them? I'm surprised you could think it even for a moment.'

His tone was severe. It was only what Paddy had said, back on John's, but Ralph knew much more. I said: 'I'm sorry.'

'And the old ruins are forbidden places, so what were you up to, prying in them?' I had no answer, and kept silent. 'You're a good lad, Ben, with good prospects, but you've lacked a proper rearing. You've much to learn.' I nodded submissively. 'Where did you get that knife I saw you playing with yesterday?'

'I bought it in the market.'

'It comes from the old time. All those gadgets: it's like a machine, almost. Better get rid of it. D'you have it with you now?'

'I left it in my room.'

'Then get shot of it as soon as you get back. Things from the old time are like gypsy goods. They're tainted. Best have no truck with any of them.'

He twitched the rein to walk his horse on. As I followed on Hussar, I felt the bulge in my trouser pocket surreptitiously. If I'd admitted having the knife with me he would have made me throw it away there and then. Liking and respecting Ralph as I did, I didn't enjoy lying to him; but I wasn't quite prepared for that.

Coming away from the following week's Summoning, I found myself staying close to Mother Ryan, and noticed Paddy did as well. I'd thought the Demons might be less terrifying on second viewing but they weren't: if anything, more so. The dinner gong would not be sounded for a while yet, and I was glad when she suggested going to her room.

She shut a window that had been left open and pulled her black shawl round her shoulders. I flopped on her bed.

'It's turned cold,' she said, but I knew it wasn't just the weather. I said: 'You could ring to have a fire lit.'

'At this hour?'

'The maid wouldn't mind.'

'But I would. It's maybe from being a servant myself, but I couldn't impose that way.'

Paddy who had taken the second chair said: 'Antonia had a fire lit in her room last night.'

'That's for her to choose.' Mother Ryan shook her head. 'It's a funny life but I suppose we needs get used to it. It could get stranger still.'

'You mean, when Antonia and Ralph get married?' Paddy asked.

'And what would you know of that?' Mother Ryan asked sharply. 'What has she said to you?'

'Nothing. But I've got eyes, haven't I?'

'Eyes indeed and ears, but you've also a tongue you must learn to curb. Nothing's happened that's proper occasion for talk. And you'll keep your mouth shut too, Ben, will ye not? What's to be will be, but we'll not look to crossing bridges till we get to them.'

I couldn't account for the lack of enthusiasm in her voice. 'What's wrong with Ralph?'

'Ralph takes Ben out riding,' Paddy said sarcastically. 'Ralph is Ben's best friend.'

Mother Ryan rubbed her hands. 'There's nought wrong with Ralph that I know of – with any of them. But we're not their kind, and they're not ours. All this of Summonings and Demons . . . I had enough of that in the old days in Ireland. God be thanked, there was little of the sort in the Isles.'

'But there is here,' I said. 'You've seen the Demons, like we have. You saw the Master's house burned down. It's no good pretending they don't exist. And they only punish the wicked – the Summoner said so.'

'And who are the wicked?' Mother Ryan asked. 'Was your poor mother wicked, when she was burnt in her bed?'

79

For a moment I had nothing to say: it was not a story I wanted to call to mind. But I felt it was unfair of her to use it in criticism of the landsmen. I said:

'It wasn't the Demons that set fire to the castle. You told me: it was men and women of her village.'

She sighed. 'And if one knew where Demons ended and men and women began, one might be more at peace.'

Much as I loved her, there were times when she didn't make sense. Demons were Demons, people people. I was prepared to continue the argument when, after a peremptory knock, her door was opened, and Millicent came in. Although the plump one of the General's two daughters, she was, I thought, the sourer. Wasting no time on civilities, she asked Mother Ryan:

'Have you seen Ralph? The Mistress wants him.'

'I saw him at the Summoning,' Mother Ryan said.

We had also seen him on the way back, talking earnestly to Antonia. I was wondering why she didn't mention that when Millicent turned to Paddy and me.

'What about you two?'

On the point of speaking, I saw Mother Ryan's warning eye behind Millicent's back. I shook my head. Paddy said:

'I *thought* I saw him going towards the stables.'

'The Mistress expects him to come to her after the Summoning.' Millicent pursed her lips. 'I've been to Antonia's room, and she's not there.' She paused, but none of us spoke. 'If you see him, tell him his mother wishes to see him, at once.' Then she left us.

On Monday morning I was up early. Ralph was making me a kite and had promised we could try it out. The weather was still unsettled and a brisk south-easterly promised perfect conditions. I found him in the stables where we usually met, but checking the saddle of his horse. He told me he had business in the town which had to be attended to. He seemed preoccupied, but when I showed my disappointment ruffled my hair and smiled.

'I've made you the kite, though. Try it on your own. If you've any problems, I'll sort them out when I get back.'

I was doing as he suggested when, later in the morning, I saw Heron approaching across the carefully shaven turf of the main lawn. He was the head servant, tall and stooped, with a bony face and drooping white moustache. I guessed he was looking for one of the gardeners, but he stopped beside me.

In a creaking voice, he said: 'You are required in the courtyard, young sir.'

I nodded, and concentrated on the kite. I'd had problems in getting it fully airborne, but it was now straining high against the wind. Heron repeated:

'You are required in the courtyard. At once. By the General.'

I wound the kite in, and followed him. General Pengelly, together with the Mistress and Rachel and Millicent, was standing by the fish pond. I had an impression that he looked strange – nervous? – but dismissed it. The Mistress' face was blank, her lips tightly drawn.

Facing them across the pond were Mother Ryan, Antonia and Paddy. As I joined them, the General said:

'Although this does not concern you, Ben, I thought you should be present. You may go, Heron.'

Paddy looked sullen, Mother Ryan wary. I could not read Antonia's expression. Addressing them, the General said:

'You have been with us how long – two weeks? Sheriff Wilson sent you away from the Western Isles because you were not native to his territory. We have been considering your position since then. It is known to be the will of the

Dark One that people should cleave to the land of their birth. Since you came from Ireland, it is right you should return to that country.'

Antonia's face was pale. In a low voice, Mother Ryan asked: 'How soon, sir?'

'At once. There is no point in delay.'

'And when does the next boat sail?'

'You will not be taken by boat. You are to go by road to a port in the north, and sail from there. You must be ready to leave by two o'clock this afternoon.'

He sounded relieved to have got it over. Mother Ryan asked:

'Shall we take our leave of Ralph first?'

While he hesitated, the Mistress spoke sharply. 'That will not be possible. *Master* Ralph will be engaged in the town for the entire day.'

The two women locked gazes for a long moment, before Mother Ryan turned away. 'Come, children,' she said. 'We have our packing to do.'

All this had taken me by surprise: not until this moment did I grasp that it was serious – that Mother Ryan and the girls were actually being banished from the place in which they had hitherto seemed entirely welcome. I said:

'They don't have to go to Ireland.' I caught the Mistress' eye, and quickly added: '. . . sir. I can go back to the Western Isles as Sheriff Wilson wanted, and take them with me. He said I could.'

The General looked past me to Mother Ryan. 'As you have said, you have packing to do.' He turned to me. 'You will remain here, Ben.'

When I rejoined the others, in Mother Ryan's room, she was tightening the string of her draw-bag. Her smile was warm as always, but there was unhappiness in it.

'What did they say to you?'

I was troubled, and also confused. 'The General said it made no difference what Sheriff Wilson said. The will of the Dark One has to be obeyed. I said in that case I wanted to go with you, to Ireland. But he won't let me.'

'Well, I suppose that's no great surprise, since you're to be the new Master.'

Her words made me wince. They echoed those of the General in refusing my request. I had an inheritance here, he had said, and responsibilities. In answer, I'd said if that were so I would do as the Sheriff suggested and go back to the Western Isles. I was thinking it might be possible to send to Ireland for them after that. The will of the Dark One had been misinterpreted once already, and if the Sheriff wanted to keep me there *his* Summoner might take a different view from the General's.

The General reluctantly agreed that a message could be sent to Sheriff Wilson, if I wished; but it would take several days to get a reply. I asked if the departure of Mother Ryan and the girls could be put off until then. The Mistress intervened before the General could respond. That was out of the question, she said. Her look registered total contempt for all males, whether Generals or Masters. The business was settled: I had better go and bid my friends good-bye.

I said to Mother Ryan: 'I don't see why you have to go today. I spoke to one of the guards, who's on dock duty. There's a boat to Ireland from here next week. Even if it is the Dark One's will, what difference can a few days make? We've been here longer than that already.'

It was Paddy who answered, bitterly. 'Don't you see it's not the General who's deciding? It's *her*. It might be awkward for her little boy if we were allowed to stay on.'

I was puzzled. 'What little boy?'

'Ralph, you idiot. It was him being soft on Antonia that

got us here in the first place. And that's the reason for us being sent away before he gets back.'

Mother Ryan said: 'Paddy . . .'

'Oh, why not admit it! Antonia knows the truth. His mother was willing to overlook it as long as it wasn't serious – just another little titbit for him. But when he went walking with Antonia after the Summoning, instead of going to her, it was a different matter. A girl from the islands couldn't possibly be suitable as a wife for her wonderful son, so she decided to put a stop to it. And we're being packed off before he gets back so he doesn't have to face any embarrassment.'

She was angry, and she was being unreasonable. I said: 'But when Ralph does get back, this evening . . .'

'We'll be gone,' Paddy said wearily. 'That's what I'm trying to tell you.'

'You'll not have gone far. Ralph will come for you.'

'You don't understand.'

She spoke as though she were not just a year and a bit but ten years older. She was the one who didn't understand. Antonia was silently staring out of the window. The prettiness I'd noticed had vanished: she looked plain and tired. I remembered her with the yellow flowers round her, saying she wouldn't mind if she never lived anywhere else but here. I thought of all the times she had teased me too, cruelly sometimes, and even wished them back.

Mother Ryan put her arms round me. 'We've had good days together. Now you're growing up. You're going to be all right. And there has to be a time for parting.'

'It won't be for long. Ralph will bring you back.'

Her smile was weary. 'Maybe. Or maybe you'll send for us, when you've your new house built on the isle. Take care, lovey.'

★

84

I went looking for Ralph after I saw a groom leading his horse to the stables. Eventually I discovered him in his room, an unlikely place for him to be while daylight lingered. He was lying on his bed, staring at the ceiling.

I plunged into an account of what had happened. I had no doubt that he would be indignant, and eager to put things right. But he made no move, did not even look at me, and I found myself stumbling over my words. I wound up, doggedly:

'They weren't on the road till nearly four. They can't have gone much more than a dozen miles.'

I'd been hoping he would take me with him – had envisaged us riding together through the night until we reached them. I'd pictured Paddy's face when she saw us. When he did finally turn to me though, his look was blank. He said, in a closed-up kind of voice:

'There's nothing to be done. I'm sorry, Ben.'

'But there is! It was your mother's idea to send them away, not the General's. And she'll let you have whatever you want: she always does. You want to marry Antonia, don't you?'

'People can't always have what they want. It's something you'll learn.'

I couldn't believe what he was saying. 'But at least you can help people you're fond of, can't you? Not simply stand by when they're treated badly.'

I realized I was being reckless, even impertinent, and thought he might be angry. He swung his legs off the bed, but only said in a dull voice:

'You just don't see, Ben. You don't think I'm happy about it, do you? But there has to be order, and rules, and people must learn to obey them. During the Madness people did as they liked, and all they got from it was murder and misery.'

'But just because your mother thinks . . .'

Ralph stood up. 'There's no point in discussing it. What's done is done. Do you think there's enough light still for me to show you a few tricks with that kite?'

I thought of the old man in the tent. 'Landsmen are dogs, ready to snarl or wag tail as their masters bid them.' Masters; or mothers.

'No,' I said. 'It's too dark.'

They were nice to me at dinner. Both Millicent and Rachel went out of their way to talk to me, and even the Mistress managed a smile or two. Nothing was said of the three faces missing from the table. Ralph excused himself early, but before going suggested we ride out to Middlebrook Farm in the morning, to see if any more cows had gone down with milk fever. Then he went to kiss his mother good night.

The villa seemed very empty, and I went early to my room. I kept thinking Paddy would burst in, or Mother Ryan call me. I wondered where they had stopped for the night, and how they were.

I tried to look on the bright side. That everyone here was being nice was confirmation of the fact of my inheritance. Once that was properly secured, things would be different. As Master, I would have power – power perhaps to bring them back, to the islands. The Dark One might be the ruler of the universe, but his rulings, I was beginning to understand, were interpreted by ordinary human beings. They could make mistakes, and they could also be persuaded.

It wasn't something that could be done straight away, of course. It would take time. Things needed to be done in order. It might be months before I could manage it, a year maybe.

'There has to be order and rules . . .' Suddenly, and shockingly, my line of thought disgusted me. I was thinking like Ralph – like a landsman.

I slept fitfully and was awake very early. No one was about as I took Hussar from his stall, saddled and mounted him. A few birds were beginning to call from hedgerows as I reached the fork by the mill and headed north, towards Paddy and Mother Ryan and Antonia.

I was a bit light-headed, but much happier. Reaching a hand into my pocket I touched the knife: at least I had not been such a fool as to obey that particular instruction from Ralph. I set Hussar to a canter and something else metallic slapped against my chest. I felt inside my shirt, and drew out the medallion. The symbol of my inheritance, Sheriff Wilson had said, to be kept with me always. But what was that inheritance worth, when it came attached to strings that could be pulled by Sheriff Wilson or General Pengelly – or by his wife?

Without Mother Ryan and Antonia – without Paddy – it was meaningless, a nothing. As I rose, I eased the chain over my head and held the medallion in my hand. Perhaps it had signified something to my father, but it had no value for me. Rising in the saddle, I drew back my arm and threw it as far as I could.

The day brightened, and I could see the surrounding country more clearly. To my right it was thickly wooded, but on the other side open fields stretched away. Men were already at work there: heads briefly lifted before bending again to labour. Any horseback rider must be gentry, and the ways of the gentry were beyond either their reckoning or interest.

Not until the sun was above the trees did I see anyone on the road itself: an approaching speck which gradually became a figure. The figure was on foot, which meant there was no cause for alarm. When the traveller turned off the road and headed into the fields, I guessed it was someone from an outlying village, perhaps taking breakfast to one of the labourers.

Yet there was no one working near, and the figure's movements seemed odd. Having distanced himself from the road, he was proceeding parallel to it. He – or she? I first saw it was a girl, and then recognized not the distant blur of features but a familiar spring in the walk. Paddy!

When I spurred towards her she began running further in to the field. I called her name several times before she stopped. I slipped from the saddle, leaving reins dangling, and ran to hug her.

Interrupting one another, we exchanged explanations. She had sneaked off while the rest were asleep, not sure what she would do when she got to the villa but determined to get me away as she had done before. I simply said I'd decided to go after them. I didn't speak of Ralph, and she asked no questions.

I led Hussar back to the road and we both got up, with Paddy in the saddle and me perched awkwardly in front. With such a load we could look for no better than walking pace, but Paddy said the wagon's progress had been still slower. They would have spent time looking for her too, and might not yet have resumed their journey north. We should have no great difficulty in catching up with them.

I asked: 'What will the guards say, when you turn up with me?'

She shrugged. 'We'll tell them something.'

Her confidence was infectious, we were back together, and the morning was bright. And the guards were landsmen, used to doing as they were told. They'd been ordered to take a party north, and a fourth would make little difference.

The fields tailed away into barren land and scrub, empty of houses. On the other side though, we spied habitation. They were screened by trees, which accounted for Paddy not having seen them on her journey south, but in daylight the line of covered wagons was plainly visible. Smoke rose from camp fires. I heard children's cries, and a barking dog.

'Gypsies!' I whispered. Paddy nodded, urging Hussar to a slightly brisker pace. We did not appear to have been seen and the voices soon faded, along with the smell of wood-smoke. After a long stretch of road we were coming to a bend. I looked back, to make sure no-one from the camp was following, and saw a cloud of dust in the distance.

Perhaps foolishly I had given no thought to being pursued. I was a guest, the General had said, and a guest is someone who can leave as and when he chooses. For that matter, what reason could there be for seeking to keep me against my will? It made no difference to the General who was Master of Old Isle. But I knew at once the cloud marked a troop of horse, and with equal certainty knew their mission was to capture the departing guest, and take him back as a prisoner.

They were out of sight as we rounded the bend, but less than half a mile away. We scrambled off Hussar, and Paddy whacked his buttock: he whinnied in protest, and galloped off. We took shelter in brush at the side of the road as Pengelly's men cantered past.

Paddy gripped my arm. 'They'll double back when they find him riderless. Better run for it.'

It was hard and painful going. The ground rose to a ridge, then dipped towards an edge of woodland that promised better cover. That was where Paddy stumbled and fell. I helped her up and she said she was all right, but winced when she put her foot to the ground. Teeth gritted, she said:

'Come *on*! They'll have caught him by now.'

But she was limping badly, and we were in heavy undergrowth. I went ahead, pushing aside branches to make it easier for her. With relief I saw open space before us.

It was not until I had broken through into the clearing that I noticed something else: a man standing directly in our path, with a gun in the crook of his arm.

7

He was squat, not much taller than I was, but powerfully built: broad-chested, the arm that cradled the gun strongly muscled. He wore a leather jerkin over a coarse grey shirt whose sleeves were rolled high, and leather trousers and sandals. Arms and face were dark-brown from exposure to sun, and wrinkled by age and weather. He had a wide ugly face with dark, deep-set eyes and a splayed nose, and a scar ran from his right eye to the corner of his mouth. He had shaved, but not recently: a stubble of grey beard matched the loose strands that failed to cover his brown bald head. His mouth opened in a gappy smile, but the teeth remaining were strong and white.

'Now then, me darlins,' he said in a gravelly voice. 'What's wi' ye?'

Neither of us replied. So close to their camp, he must be a gypsy. A dirty lot, Ralph had said: thieves, maybe still infected with the Madness. According to the country people, they could lay spells. Steer clear of them, Ralph had warned.

There was also the gun. It wasn't like the guns Pengelly's soldiers carried; it seemed older, and was double-barrelled. His right hand held it just beneath the trigger-guard and the barrels caught a flash of sunlight.

'It were pigeon I were after,' he went on, 'but I had an eye to the road. What I seed there was two young 'uns riding the one pony, and early in the day to be so far from a sassenach dwelling. Then comes a dozen or more riders, goin' lickety-split. And now I finds the same two young 'uns runnin' hard through the brush.'

He fixed a half-closed eye on us. 'What did ye do with the horse? Set him loose? He looked a beast worth keeping, except they'd run ye down quick if ye stayed with him. Ye're in trouble, I'd say.'

'We're all right,' Paddy said. The calmness of her voice impressed me. 'We don't need help, thank you.'

He made no immediate reply – in fact looked away, cocking his head as though listening. All I could hear was a blackbird, and the coo of a pigeon. He had said he'd come out after pigeon. 'They've struck back,' he said, after a moment. 'They're off the road and beating this way. Four of 'em, at least. Even without one of ye bein' lame, they'd ketch ye within a half hour. As it is, five minutes.'

He spoke with flat certainty. Paddy's eyes met mine. If we were caught, nothing too bad was likely to happen; but Paddy would certainly be sent on to join the others and I would be kept at the villa, probably under guard. I wouldn't be given a second chance to walk away.

'Hearken,' the gypsy said.

Now I could hear it: distant feet, trampling through undergrowth.

'Can you hide us?' I asked.

He shook his ugly head. 'Not here. Not nowhere in the woods. They'd be bound to hit on ye, sooner or later.'

I realized he had not actually offered the help Paddy had refused. Perhaps he had just been mocking us. Or getting us off guard while he considered the best way of handing us over? He might be counting on a reward.

'Nowhere in the woods,' he repeated. 'But sassenachs won't come nigh our caravans. Feared of goin' mad, as

I've heard.' He grinned widely. 'Which are ye more feared of – the mad didikoi, or gettin' ketched?'

'We'll go with you,' Paddy said quickly.

'So be.' He listened again. 'They're comin' on fast. I'll carry ye, missy, with your permission. You follow, boy, and see can ye out-run me.'

There was small chance of that. He picked up Paddy with his free arm and swung her easily over his shoulder; then set off in a loping run, breaking through bushes he could not easily skirt. I followed, marvelling at the pace he set.

Dogs barked as we approached the camp, and other gypsies looked at us, but with no particular sign of interest. Children went on playing in the dust. There were six painted wagons, and he headed for one at the end, a little apart from the others. Its door was approached by wooden steps; he lowered Paddy and pushed us inside. Following, he closed the lower half of the door and leaned on it, gazing out.

It was dim inside the wagon and there was a variety of smells, not all pleasant. From outside came sounds of whistling, a howling dog, people talking. Later we heard more distant voices, calling one another. That went on for about ten minutes, but it was as long again before the gypsy turned to us.

'They're gone. I doubt they'll come back, but ye'd be wise not to venture abroad a while yet. Ye can call me Mordecai. What am I to be naming ye?'

The wagons housed more than forty gypsies. The rest were crammed with adults and children (who slept in hammocks, slung from the roof at night and packed away each morning); only Mordecai had a caravan to himself. I thought at first he might be the chief, but learned the real chief lived in a yellow and blue caravan, slightly bigger than the rest, along with his mother, his wife, their son, *his* wife, and four small children.

Mordecai asked if we were hungry, and when we admitted it left us to get food. Paddy took off her shoe and stocking and gingerly flexed her foot. I asked:

'Is it bad?'

'Bad enough.' She grimaced. 'And it's swelling.'

I thought of our situation: in the middle of nowhere, Paddy lame and Hussar on the way back to his stable. I guessed Paddy's thoughts were running on similar lines. She said, in a depressed tone:

'It was supposed to be a five-day journey north to the port, but from there boats sail to Ireland almost every day. It won't be easy now to catch up with them.'

'The gypsies have horses. If we . . .'

'Stole a couple? Not a very nice way of paying him back for hiding us.' She added practically: 'Anyway, they'd soon catch us, and what then? Horses are probably the most precious things they own.' She put weight on her foot, and winced. 'I hope this doesn't lay me up for long.'

Mordecai returned, bringing plates heaped with bacon, eggs and sausages. Also what looked like mushrooms, but darker in colour and differently shaped. I left these till last, and saw him watching me.

'D'ye think they've gypsy poison in 'em?'

He took a fork, speared and ate one, smacking his lips. 'What are they?' I asked. 'Not mushrooms.'

'It bein' this time o' year, ye mean? There are more godsends in woods and meadows than sassenachs know. Morels come in spring and early summer, when the world's ripening.'

'They're delicious,' Paddy said. 'Better than mushrooms.'

I tried them, and they were. Mordecai took away the

94

plates, and returned with battered mugs of a hot liquid whose taste was strange but refreshing.

'Now,' he said, scratching the stubble of his beard. 'What's to be done wi' ye? It might be a help to know what ye're about, and why the sassenachs were chasing ye, but a man's business is his own till such a time as he chooses to share it.'

Ignoring a look from Paddy, I told him something of what had happened. Not all. I didn't mention Ralph or the Master; only spoke of being banished from the Isles, of Mother Ryan and the girls being sent on further, and the events of the past few hours.

'So it's Ireland ye'll be lookin' to go to?'

'Yes.'

'And ye've lost your horse, and it's a tidy step to the port even for them as is fit for walking.'

He stopped for what I imagined would be a moment's consideration; but the pause lengthened. As he stared out of the caravan, I watched cloud slowly obscure the semi-circle of sky, and as slowly clear again. I had a feeling his mind was somewhere else – that in this interval we did not exist for him.

In the beginning this created an awkwardness, but that lessened as time went by. I took stock of our surroundings, which were not as cluttered as I had first thought. Certainly the caravan was tightly packed – with pans, plates, buckets, fishing rods and nets and gaffs, a range of tools (all clean and polished), boxes and sacks, strings of dried plants . . . but each thing seemed to be in its proper place, and there was an overall impression of tidiness.

Eventually Mordecai turned to us, his face relaxing into its gap-toothed grin.

'So it's Ireland ye seek – by way of the north port? We didikoi are travellers, as maybe ye've heard. We make our way from place to place, accordin' to the season and following old paths. Just now, we're heading north. If ye'd wish to travel with us, ye're welcome.'

He did not wait for a response but went out. We heard his footsteps pad away. Paddy looked at me.

I said: 'Well?'

'Rachel said gypsies stole children. I can't think why, when they've so many of their own. Millicent said there were stories that they fattened them up, and ate them. I'd have thought stealing a pig would be less trouble.'

'Taste better too, I should think.'

We laughed. I said: 'What about the Madness?'

'If it's anything like mumps or measles, we've probably caught it already. But Mordecai doesn't look mad.'

'Your foot really has swollen.'

'Yes.' She prodded it gently. 'Right now I doubt if I could crawl.'

'So we might as well hang on with them, at least until it's better.'

She nodded. 'We're headed in the right direction. We've no chance anyway of catching up on this side of the water.' She shook her head. 'I'd still like to know *why* he suggested our staying.'

Before I had time to respond to that, we heard Mordecai returning. This time he brought a bowl of hot water with herbs floating in it, and set it down by Paddy.

'Rest your foot in that, me beauty. Ye'll find 'twill ease and heal it both.'

Paddy said: 'Mr Mordecai . . .'

'No misters here, lassie. Nor Generals, nor servants. Mordecai, it is.'

'We'd like to stay, Mordecai. Thank you very much.'

Next morning that camp was abandoned, and the caravans

moved on. Progress was leisurely, limited by the pace of a laden donkey or a child-herded goat: one could forage afield and catch up easily. After several days of unhurried travel, a new resting place was found. It was in a hollow, half a mile from the road: a dell with a stream running through, and at the bottom a rocky pool where the women washed the family clothes, beating them clean against boulders. It was plainly an accustomed staging point in their processions, and one of the first jobs for the children was to root out saplings and bushes which had encroached since the previous year. Paddy and I took a hand without being told: we had learned that with gypsies you did not need to ask or be asked. People knew what was expected of them, and set about it with a will.

Paddy's ankle was fully recovered. Resting after our labours, chewing grass shoots in the sunshine, she said: 'They'll be in Ireland by this time. I wonder what it's like. I don't remember anything of it.'

I certainly didn't. I asked: 'Do you think we ought to leave the gypsies and get on faster?'

She considered that. 'We're safer with them, if anyone's still looking for us. And I suppose there's no particular hurry now.'

I wouldn't have argued if she had said yes, but was happier that she didn't. I was getting to know the other members of the tribe, and the solemn warnings about gypsies already seemed laughable. At night we slept snug in blankets beneath Mordecai's caravan; by day chatted with him as the convoy followed its deliberate course. He had a great store of knowledge of country life and ways, and seemed happy to impart it. Also, he had promised to take me hunting as soon as there was an opportunity.

The following afternoon in fact, shotgun under his arm, he took the two of us into the wood that surrounded the new camp. Then and during similar expeditions, he showed us how to listen and how to look – neither as simple as they first seemed – for what was needed: food for the cooking pot, both animal and vegetable. He taught us ways of reading spoors and droppings, not just which beast had left them – deer or rabbit, fox or badger or wild pig – but the wherefore as well as what: the creature's size, and age, and condition.

And he taught us how to move in the wild – slowly, quietly, surely – and how to read wind and weather and use them in our stalking.

'Everything ye do,' he told us, 'needs thinking through aforehand: careful and clear and honest.'

It took time as well as patience. We returned that day with only a small bag, a couple of rabbits, but the beginning of new knowledge. It was knowledge not merely of the practicalities but of the laws of the hunter's life and the discipline of the gun; based on its fearful power, which enforced a duty to kill from need only, and cleanly. Economically too. Ammunition was not easily replaced.

That evening, as we picked the bones of roast rabbit, I asked Mordecai about Demons. He drew on his pipe, which had a creamy white stem that shaded to dark brown around the bowl, the bowl itself being carved in the shape of a woman's head.

'What of them, laddy?'

'You never go to Summonings, do you?'

He took the pipe from his mouth to shake out dottle. 'Never been asked.'

'We weren't *asked*. Just told.'

'Never been told, neether.'

'The Summoners say Demons hunt down people who don't attend. Aren't you frightened they might come after you?'

'Not in partic'lar.' He rammed in fresh tobacco, out of a battered jar with a picture on the side of a woman wearing a crown. 'Them sassenachs you've been living among — you ever hear them talk of being frightened by wolves?'

'No.'

'That's a-cause there ain't any wolves in southern woods. Up in northern forests, it's a different tale: you get wolves there, and bear too for that matter. Not that wolves do any harm — keep to themselves, do wolves — but the northern sassenachs worry lest they take their children.' He grinned. 'Barring the gypsies don't ketch 'em first! Now bear's another case altogether. You needs keep a sharp look-out for bear.'

Paddy said: 'But there *are* Demons — in the south, anyway.'

'Oh, ay?'

'We've seen them,' I said, and my flesh bristled despite the mildness of the night. Mordecai drew on his pipe.

'It's a funny thing.'

He paused, and I asked: 'What is?'

'Them sassenachs you was with, they're called the Mill people. That's on account their demons come out from the top of a mill. In the next territory going north, you get the Stack people. Their demons come from old chimney-stacks. And up in the north port there's Mast people. Theirs come out from tops of masts in old hulks at the harbour's end.'

'So what's funny about it?' Paddy asked.

'Well, I been travelling the length and breadth of this land more'n sixty years. I've seed a sight of high places, but never a demon's nest in one of 'em. It's as though they're reserved special for sassenachs. No, us didikoi don't bother demons, and demons don't bother us. Now let's talk of our proper concerns. Before you puts a gun away, you cleans it. Sit ye there, and watch the way I do it.'

I duly watched: everything Mordecai did was worth watching, and learning from. But a sense of uncertainty and confusion lingered. The fact that gypsies were not called to Summonings and that he had never seen a Demon was one thing; the fact of Demons' existence quite another. Having seen them with my eyes, had my ears bombarded by their cries, it was something of which I could be certain. It puzzled me that he, so interested in everything that went on about him, should be so indifferent in this case. I recalled Mother Ryan saying the Master too had made light of Demons. How could they – in their very different ways the two wisest men I had known – have been so incurious?

I tried to tell myself it did not matter: that nothing mattered outside this good life which now embraced us. I thought of the luxury and order of Pengelly's villa, contrasting it with the rough-and-ready freedom of the gypsy way, and knew beyond doubt which I preferred. I thought too of being Master of Old Isle, a far-away, forgotten dream.

But were any of them things that really mattered? What of the aim we had been pursuing when we were saved from Pengelly's men and taken in by Mordecai: what of Mother Ryan? Well, we were still heading in the right direction. That was something, wasn't it? I glanced at Paddy, who was leaning back looking up at a yellow moon. It was she who had said there was no particular hurry about catching up with the others. I was shamefully glad she hadn't brought the subject up again.

It was a summer of sustained good weather, warm even by the standard of the Western Isles. Morning after morning we were wakened by the sun's rays slanting under the caravan as the year matured, day by leafy day. Cherries and gooseberries ripened, and strawberries, raspberries, plums, pears and apples followed in tempting succession. Some of these fruits grew wild, but I fear more came out of gardens and orchards. Several times we were chased by angry sassenachs (as we too came to call them), twice nearly caught. 'Thieving gypsies!' they yelled after us as we legged it with our spoils.

At the beginning I thought occasionally of Sheriff Wilson's words in the General's office: 'We found you . . . will always find you, wherever you may be'. He had sounded confident. But as the days passed both the threat and recollection of the Sheriff himself grew shadowy. I felt safe in a green wilderness.

We grew to know the other gypsies, discovering them to be ordinary people, neither specially good nor bad. Marie, for instance, was a scold, as quick to turn her razor-edge tongue on us as on her own three children. Petey was a sot: the gypsies made their own liquor and apart from him used it moderately. He was more noisy when drunk than Andy had been, and the first time we witnessed him ranting and falling about was alarming, but we grew used to it. He did no harm.

Neddo was the tribe's chief, though it was his mother, Gypsy Granny, who commanded most respect. She was very small, brown and wrinkled like a walnut, and fearsome when crossed. I gave offence in the first week by making too much noise near their caravan while she was having her afternoon nap; and thereafter thought it best to steer clear of her. But she took a fancy to Paddy, and Paddy to her.

She hauled me in also one afternoon, to help prepare black currants for a pie. (At each camp, Neddo made a clay oven, around which embers were skilfully packed, for the tribe's baking). This was a tedious job, which she supervised with eyes that, however old, were relentlessly sharp for tops and tails not as neatly snipped as she demanded.

When we had finished she brought out little maids-of-honour cakes, and rich sweet herb tea in big china mugs. And after we'd drunk the tea, she read the leaves and told our fortunes. Paddy, she pronounced, would marry a tall dark man, and have seven children. When it was my turn, she stared into the mug a long time before speaking.

'It's a far land,' she said at last. 'And full of strange sights. Wagons that fly, pictures coming out of the air. I see you made much of.' She shrugged. 'Beyond that, nothing clear.'

I had been hostile even before she turned her attention to me. 'Do the wagons have wings?' I asked. 'And feathers? What colour feathers – black, white, purple and yellow? Maybe the tall dark man has feathers too?'

I thought my boldness might anger her, but the wizened face laughed at me.

'Why, laddy, are ye not dark . . . and may grow taller? I see what I see. What would you have me say – that I see the two of ye together still?'

'We shall be.'

I spoke warmly. She smiled. 'I think ye will. For a time, anyway. Nothing is ever longer than for a time. All couples end at last, and one goes on alone.'

On our way back to Mordecai's caravan, I said:

'She's old, of course, which is why she talks nonsense.'

'Old, yes. I'm not sure about the nonsense.'

'Pictures coming out of the air!'

'And a tall dark husband for me.' Paddy laughed. 'I hope she's wrong about the seven children!'

One afternoon I sat with Mordecai under the brow of a

hill in an oak tree's shade. There had recently been a heavy shower; the smell of rain hung in the air but the sun had broken fiercely through and the grass steamed. I had been given use of the gun that day – the rheumatics were tormenting his shoulder, Mordecai said – and we had a goose and a brace of wild duck for the pot. I glowed at his commendation.

'Ye're a fair shot, laddy. There needs be a rhythm in all things, not least in duck shooting, and ye have it . . . aye, ye have it.'

Paddy had preferred to stay with Gypsy Granny. I wondered how I might convey his praise when we got back without being mocked for boasting. At least, I would be able to display my bag. I stroked the gun.

'It's very old, isn't it?'

'My father's, and my father's father's, and his great-great-grandfather's before him. From the old time, like that little knife o' yourn.'

'I was told to throw it away. He –' I could not bring myself to mention Ralph – 'said it was a kind of machine, and that machines were part of what brought the Madness.'

He shrugged. 'If ye pay little attention to ought that the sassenachs say, ye're paying too much.'

'But what did cause the Madness?'

'Who knows? Who cares? The didikoi were travelling long before the sassenachs built their tall cities, and they're still travelling now they're gone. And as to madness, look yonder.'

'What?'

We had a view south across open country. As he pointed I picked up what his keener eye had spotted: a score or more horsemen about a mile away. No longer concerned about pursuit, I regarded them with mild curiosity.

'I wonder what they're up to.'

Mordecai sucked on his pipe. 'Starting one of their wars again is my guess. It must be all of three years since they fought one another, in these parts any road. There's a war up north that's lasted going on ten year now.'

'Why *do* they fight?' I asked.

It was a question that would not have occurred to me before living with the gypsies. War between territories was taken for granted, even in the Western Isles which were too remote to be involved.

'Why do a fox kill fifty chickens in a pen, when a brace'll serve for him and his wife and pups an' all? While a hawk kills once, and clean. The sassenachs sit under roofs, peaceable and quiet, till the mood comes on 'em to start slaughtering one another. 'Tis part of the contrarities of nature, and past man's understanding. All we didikoi need do is go about our business, and pay'm no heed.'

He stood up, knocking his pipe against the trunk of the oak.

'I know a pool down the bottom yer that mostly harbours a few fat trout. I'll learn ye the way of tickling 'em out.'

Suddenly, as though exhausted by the effort it had made, the summer turned grey. Leaves yellowed and fell, spinning down on a stiffening breeze. We had been camped more than a week, and there was a sense of impending movement.

After breakfast, on a dry bleak morning, Mordecai said:

'We're off today. And not far along we'll be turnin' to go east.'

He did not need to spell out what that meant: they would be no longer following the road that led to the north port. He got up from his seat.

'I've things to see to.'

I did not look at Paddy as he padded down the steps of the caravan. The everyday sounds of the gypsy encampment surrounded us, but here inside there was a silence that was stifling. I wanted to break it, but did not know how. I felt she ought to say something, and was irritated that she didn't. In the end, I said:

'This is not the only road north. I asked Petey. There are places further on where you can branch off towards the port.'

She still did not speak. I turned to her, willing her to say something. Her expression was unhappy, but she also had a stubborn look I knew well.

'It's true,' I insisted. 'Several places.'

She said at last, in a tight voice: 'We'd be going away from the port. And making it a longer journey when we did turn back. If we turned back.'

The tone hinted doubt even more than the words. She was implying I was wavering from our intention of following Mother Ryan and Antonia to Ireland. I was angry with her for suggesting such a thing, while realizing it was true. I said, aware of the prickle in my voice:

'Anyway, there's no hurry. They'll have been in Ireland for weeks already – months. What difference does a week or two more following them make?'

Yet I knew I was not really talking about a week or two. I was happy here with Mordecai, and did not want to leave at all. After the first week, there would be another, and another.

Paddy said: 'We should have left sooner – as soon as my ankle was better. That was my fault, but now . . . You do as you think best. I'm going north.'

'You can't.' She looked at me coldly. 'Not on your own.'

'On my own?' Her expression turned into one of angry amazement. 'You mean, I need *you*? That really is funny.' She got up and headed for the door. 'Do as you like – I'm following Mother and Antonia, as I said I would.'

My own anger simmered when I was left alone. If she'd asked me to go with her it might have been different, but I didn't see why I should be coerced. She had treated the notion of needing me with contempt, so she could get on with it. Why should I leave Mordecai and the gypsies just because she said so?

But lacking the fuel of opposition, gradually anger cooled. Recollection cooled it more: she had left Mother Ryan and Antonia and come back to help me, just as she had helped me when I was Sheriff Wilson's prisoner. There were other memories too, memories of Mother Ryan herself . . . bandaging a gashed arm, comforting me as she put a cold compress on a fevered brow, rescuing me from the uncontrollable panic of nightmare. Mordecai had proved a good friend, but she had been there from the beginning.

This was a good life; but I could not go on living it without abandoning something more important. I went to the door of the caravan, and called Paddy.

Mordecai simply nodded when I told him.

'Ye have a path of your own, and a duty, as all men have. Time's ripe to follow both. Stay on this road beyond the crossroads and ye'll fetch up at the port in three days – two if ye don't dawdle.'

I resented his casual acceptance. I had been hoping he might express regret, maybe even say something to provide a reason for reconsidering the decision. I said, almost fretfully:

'Why do you have to go east anyway? Because you always have? What's wrong with doing things differently now and then?'

'We're travellers,' he said, 'and we travel a known path. We always have, always will. It's our way, and we knows no better.'

He spoke as though from a distance. I could have argued, but bit it back. Although he had taken us in, and been good to us, it might be a relief to see us go. He was a gypsy, an old man set in his ways. We had perhaps been a nuisance to someone so long accustomed to living by himself. We were not his kind, after all.

At the crossroads we took the road north, not looking back. We had been given back-packs with rations, and a billycan for brewing tea, and Paddy was carrying something in a long deerskin pouch. A present from Gypsy Granny, I assumed, but was not inclined to ask about it. Or to speak at all. We plodded on in silence for hours before stopping to eat. It was Paddy who finally burst out:

'It's not just you, you know. I feel miserable as well. More maybe.' I said nothing, feeling there was nothing to say. 'About Mordecai. But she made me promise not to tell you till we'd left them.'

'She – you mean Gypsy Granny?' I asked indifferently. 'Tell me what?'

'Remember, at the beginning, we wondered about him being on his own, when the rest all belonged to families? He wasn't always. When he was younger, much younger, he had a wife and two children.'

'Well?'

'There was a storm one winter, when they were camped near a river. A flood carried his caravan away. He tried to save them, but couldn't. The others dragged him out.'

I felt a tightness in my chest that was also a fullness.

'The children ... were they a boy and a girl?' She nodded. 'You should have told me!'

'She said I wasn't to – that it would do no good. He's

not spoken about it since it happened, and wouldn't want it spoken of now. She was right. She's a wise woman.'

Between anger and jealousy, and a parching sadness, I said: 'I know you thought so. She favoured you, didn't she? The wise old woman . . . with her crazy talk!' I flicked a finger towards the pouch lying beside her. 'What's that she gave you – a magic broom, to fly on?'

Paddy shook her head. 'It wasn't Gypsy Granny who gave it to me. Mordecai did, to give to you.' She picked it up. 'Here. I'll be glad to be rid of carrying it.'

The moment she said that I knew what it was. Anger was swallowed up by sadness, and I felt dry and cold and shivery. I said, tight-voiced: 'I don't want it. It's his. His! I'll take it back to him.'

'No.'

'They travel slowly. I can be there by nightfall if I hurry.'

'Ben, no.' There was more gentleness than usual in her voice. 'He said to tell you his shooting days are finished, and he wants you to have it. And he said to tell you: don't come back. Some roads are for retracing, he said, but some are for treading only once.'

I could hear him saying it, in his gravelly voice. After a long while, I said:

'Let's go, then. He told us not to dawdle.'

8

In the early afternoon we came to a village, and made a detour round it. We were much further north and searches must long since have been called off, but it made no sense to take chances. By the time we got back to the road it was starting to rain. Trees nearby were still in good leaf, and I suggested sheltering beneath them.

Paddy said: 'It's not really raining.'

The drops which starred the dust were heavy but sporadic, the sky uncertain. Heavy clouds were banked in the west, but the wind was southerly. I said:

'I think it will soon. Heavily, too.'

She shook her head. 'If you're tired, though . . .'

Unhappy was what I was: unsure and out of sorts. Although I had accepted Mordecai's injunction against going back, later doubts had undermined my resolution. It would not have taken long to retrace my steps, and I could have given him back the gun. Or thanked him for it. Or . . . He had said I had a duty, and duty was something I knew he took seriously; but what sort of duty were we talking about? It wasn't as though Mother Ryan was in trouble or danger. She was safe in her native land, with Antonia. I thought of the last time I'd seen her, and of her saying: 'There's a time for parting'. That had been more than a farewell – a dismissal almost. Mordecai had given me his gun: I didn't think he would make me go away again, if I did go back.

Such thoughts had been running through my head as we trudged north. I knew them to be deceptive, excuses to do what I wanted rather than what I should, but however much I put them away they kept returning. Several times I had almost decided to give in and turn back, regardless of what Paddy might say. But each decision made the parting more definite, and in the end I realized it was too late. This depressed me further, and Paddy's remark about my tiredness was a final irritation: I hefted the gun under my arm and set off at a pace I was glad to see she did not find it easy to keep up with. My legs had lengthened since leaving the Isles.

When the rain, after stopping for a time, set in heavily, it was initially a source of resentful satisfaction. We had left wooded country behind, and the road ran through grassland offering nothing in the way of cover; so that we were soon both soaked to the skin. The sky was dark, and in the sodden landscape stretching about us we were the only living things apart from a few brown and white Jacob's sheep stolidly grazing in the pelting rain.

Paddy, trailing a few paces behind, stopped, and I looked back.

'What is it?'

She held her side. 'Stitch. I'm sorry . . .'

She was shapeless and bedraggled – miserably comic. I realized I must look no better. Seeing her standing there, rain dripping off the end of her nose, it occurred to me that I might not have been just cold and wet and depressed, but also alone. At least there were two of us.

'That's all right,' I said. 'There's no hurry. It can't get any worse.'

And from that point, in fact, the situation started to improve. The rain stopped, and the air was warm enough for our clothes to dry on us, though soggy patches remained. The sky stayed livid and was darkening deeper with the approach of evening. The thought of a night in the open on wet ground was not attractive, but we found shelter before that became a serious worry. I could not imagine who could have thought it a good idea to build a cottage in the middle of nowhere, nor what purpose it might have served, but I was grateful for it.

It was now a ruin, but much of the roof had survived and in one room the floor was quite dry. Among the things I had learned from Mordecai had been ways of making a fire, and there were flint and tinder in my pack. But one also needed dry fuel. We munched a cold supper in the dark, and settled early. I called good night; and was glad to hear Paddy call it back to me.

I felt very tired, but sleep refused to come. Listening to a scrabble that might be a rat, a distant hooting that was certainly an owl, my mind was filled with memories and speculations. Too much filled: they came and went in an exhausting dance. Mordecai . . . Mother Ryan . . . Ralph . . . the Demons . . . my inheritance, so unexpectedly gained and lost and gained again, and at last abandoned . . . the Demons once more . . . I had seen and heard and been terrified by them. But Mordecai had said . . . and so the dance of thoughts went on.

When sleep finally prevailed, it took a hold which it was in no hurry to surrender. I awoke from dreaming I was on Old Isle to sunlight through an empty window frame. Yawning, I looked to where Paddy had been lying, but the place was empty. But as I started to panic I heard movement, and she appeared from the back of the cottage.

'I found dry wood,' she said, 'in a lean-to. I'm brewing tea, and I can toast what's left of the bread. There's a spring at the back where you can wash.'

★

An hour later we were ready to move: we would have been on the road sooner but Paddy insisted on tidying up. And as we finally prepared to leave, she caught my arm.

I asked impatiently: 'What is it now?'

'Listen.'

I heard the thud of hooves, from more than a single horse – many more. The shattered doorway offered a long view of empty road in the direction we had come, but we could see only a short distance the other way. We retreated and watched from a gaping window.

The sunlight that woke me had been fleeting: the day was overcast, with a stiff breeze which flapped the cloaks of the horsemen riding past. They had swords and pistols, but looked less a cavalry troop than a mounted rabble, galloping in groups of three or four, some singly. I saw no banner, but a few still wore crimson-crested helmets such as I had seen on soldiers at the villa. Most were bare-headed, all dishevelled.

More than twenty went past, and we allowed several minutes after the last had disappeared south before taking to the road. Just beyond the cottage we found a hedge of brambles, laden with juicy berries, and lingered, picking and eating them. But we had gone too far to have any hope of doubling back to the cottage when there was a new din of hoof-beats ahead. I had scarcely time to thrust the gun into the hedge before a second batch of horsemen swept round the bend and halted at their officer's command.

Unlike the first, this was a troop under discipline. They sat relaxed in their saddles, the gold and green plumes of their helmets bobbing in the wind. Their look was business-like, and I was glad I'd ditched the gun before they saw us. I had a feeling they might have acted first and thought about it afterwards.

The one who had given the order stared down at us.

'Children . . . Though the girl's well grown.' He un-sheathed his sword, and pointed it at Paddy. 'What kind of clothes do you think you're wearing?'

'Just a dress,' she said.

Gypsy Granny had made it for her. She looked tense.

'But yellow? And where's your veil?' Paddy shook her head. 'Your *veil*, girl!'

'I don't have one.'

'You're from the south, then? So what are you doing in our territory? Camp followers, I suppose . . . to that lot we've just taught a lesson about dawn raids. Well, someone else can sort it out. Borrick, Hemmings – take them back to HQ.'

'On saddlebow would that be, sir?'

'No, you fool. Walk them. And tell the Sergeant to note your time of arrival, and find some work for you. We'll have no southland slackness here.'

He led off his troop at a canter which rapidly became full gallop. Borrick, a man with a florid face and a mous-tache flaring high to cover the greater part of his cheeks, said:

'Get a move on, boy. The Lieutenant's not a man to cross, and I'm not going to cross him on your account. You too, in the yellow dress. And no veil.' He looked to his companion, shaking his head. 'You wouldn't believe it, would you?'

We had more than an hour's hard walk, urged on by Trooper Borrick with occasional suggestions of moving us faster with the point of his sword, before we reached a palisaded camp. The Lieutenant and his troop overtook us as we arrived: he had some prisoners and a couple of loose horses in tow, and looked even more pleased with himself.

After consulting a senior officer, he announced we were to be sent on to General Ramsay, whom I presumed was the ruler of this territory. It was a relief to hear we were being provided with horses for the final stage.

The camp was in open country, but it was not long before the road was lined with houses and soon we were in a town. The houses seemed more closely packed than in the south and had, I thought, a meaner look; but my view may have been influenced by the weather, which had gloomed badly. It was colder, too.

In the centre of the town, a grim building rose higher than the rest and looked out on a square about a hundred metres across. At the far side, a slim weathered tower stood more than three times higher still. There were some, Mordecai had said, whose Demons appeared from old chimney stacks. We were in the territory of the Stack people.

I could do no more than register an impression of this before our horses clattered through an arch into a court-yard. It was nothing like the courtyard at the villa: there were no lawns or gardens, nothing in any way decorative. Massive grey stone walls were studded with small ugly windows. It might have looked less forbidding on a better day, but it wasn't easy to imagine the sun ever shining on such a barrack.

We were handed over to a man in grey uniform, who locked us in a ground floor room furnished with a table and one chair, with nothing relieving the grubby brown walls except a barred window that overlooked the court-yard. From time to time figures shuffled across it, and I commented to Paddy that the women all wore black.

She nodded. 'Black hats, black dresses – black shoes, probably, if the dresses weren't too long to see them. And black coverings over their faces.'

'Veils?'

'They must be.'

We had a closer view when the guard ushered in a woman bringing food. The black dress draped her like a tent, and her hair was tucked in under a broad-brimmed hat, her face invisible behind black muslin suspended from the brim. One could not tell even whether she was old or young. She put down the tray and left without speaking.

The food was disgusting – an almost cold stew of gristly meat, disintegrating potato and slimy onion – but we were too hungry to spurn it. After that we sat and waited. Eventually the guard came back, and told us we had been summoned to the General's presence.

The room we were taken to was more than thirty metres square, and the General's chair stood on a dais against the rear wall. It was a large chair, but he needed every inch of it. He was tall and broad, and his folded hands rested on the swell of an enormous belly. One leg, in a crimson knee-high stocking, was supported on a cushioned stool. His tunic was crimson too, with short sleeves revealing plump hairy arms. His fat face sported a ginger moustache with waxed and curled ends, and his neck was heavily jowled. Yet the centre of his face, a triangle of long narrow nose, pinched mouth, small eyes set close, gave an impression of meagreness.

When we got within a couple of metres of the dais, the guard pushed me hard in the back. I staggered but kept my footing. He put both hands on my shoulders and forced me to my knees.

'No manners, eh, boy?' General Ramsay's voice was also fat: loud and hearty. 'That makes it certain you're from the south. Which town?'

'From no town, sir.' He frowned, and I went on quickly: 'From the Western Isles.'

'Ah.' He looked at me with sudden interest. 'The

Western Isles, you say? And of about the right age. Fourteen?' I nodded, and he stroked his moustache. 'A boy of fourteen from the Western Isles . . . It'll bear looking into.'

He turned to Paddy. 'As for you . . . No veil! I suppose that could be expected with a girl from the south. But I wouldn't expect even a southland wench to wear so scandalous a colour.' He stared hard. 'Nor show her legs. And as mannerless as the boy, seemingly. Were you not taught that a female curtseys to her master?'

'No,' Paddy said. 'No one has taught me that.' Her voice was stiff.

'I see.' He leaned forward, straining over his belly. 'Well, you will have chance to learn – that lesson, and others.'

He said to the guard standing behind us: 'Give her to the women to be properly dressed. And tutored. Secure the boy in one of the upper rooms. When I say secure, I mean it. You'll answer if anything goes wrong.'

Paddy was handed over to another guard and taken towards the rear of the building. I was led upstairs and installed in a room a little bigger than the first and a little less stark: it had a narrow bed as well as a chair and table, and a fireplace which, though empty, showed evidence of past fires. The guard gestured towards a bell-pull beside it.

'That's in case you need anything, but I'd think twice before you use it. Less trouble you give, less you get.'

He was a wiry little man with a thin black moustache; he cocked his head to one side as he studied me.

'Seems the General has an interest in you. I don't know what it is, but I wouldn't bank on profiting from it. He changes his mind frequent, and quick. Keep your head down, and do as you're told. That's been my policy through life, and I've seen off plenty who thought they knew better. From the Western Isles? Where's that, then?'

I explained briefly, and he shook his head. 'Can't think

why that should take his fancy. What's your name?' I told him. 'Well, Ben, why do *you* think he wants you kept so special safe?'

I said I had no idea; and didn't. I doubted if General Ramsay even knew Sheriff Wilson's name, and he was plainly no friend to Pengelly – a bitter enemy, if the routed cavalry meant anything. The guard shrugged.

'Anyway, it's nought to me. I'll not give you a hard time, so long as you give me an easy one. If not, I warn you'll know all about it. No more trouble than's necessary – that's my policy. I've always kept my head down, but I've carried no man's can; nor will a boy's.'

He moved to the window. 'You've an outside view to see the world go by. Market Day tomorrow, and a Summoning at nightfall. You'll have a good sight of the Demons.' He laughed. 'And a sight right now of what came of last week's Summoning. Never mind: they'll clear it by dusk, and freshen the air.'

I waited until he had left before going to the window. At first I could see nothing out of the ordinary: a couple of carts drawn by weary horses, people walking by, children bowling hoops, a sweeper leaning on his broom – normal sights of a normal afternoon.

But looking further off, I saw something else. At the foot of the tower there was a wooden contraption, not unlike the stocks on Sheriff's. This one though was not designed to hold its prisoner face down, but face up, staring skyward. There was someone in it now.

What was also different was the absence of the usual jeering onlookers. People in the square seemed to give that quarter a wide berth in fact. No one I saw went within thirty metres, and one man made a considerable detour to avoid it.

Realizing that, I realized something else: during the time

I had been looking out the figure that lay there had not moved. And this was not the immobility of sleep: I was staring at a corpse.

The sky continued leaden, and the wind blowing in through my cell window stayed cold. I thought of warmer and sunnier days, and of Mordecai. He had given me the gun, his own inheritance, and within a day I had lost that too. Most likely it would lie in the hedge where I had thrust it until winter stripped the bramble of leaves, and then be a lucky find for a sharp-eyed passerby.

I had the knife still, and fingered it in my pocket. I supposed I ought to be employing it in some enterprise such as cutting the lock out of the door, but did not feel inclined to try. It was a very solid-looking door.

A woman brought supper – bread and cheese and sour milk – and the guard with the thin moustache stood by while I ate. He told me he had a boy of his own, a year younger than I was.

'Joe Johnson; like his father, and grand-father before that. He's a good lad. I can tell you *he* won't get himself in trouble, traipsing off to foreign parts.'

His was not company I would have chosen under better conditions, but he seemed, apart from his callousness about the body beneath the tower and his passion for staying out of trouble, as amiable as one could expect of a landsman. He also seemed more than willing to talk, and there were things I might usefully learn. I asked about his son, and he answered with ready pride. The boy was a good runner and could use his fists. He had the makings of a guard, when he was older.

'And it's no bad job for a man.' He spoke from the window. 'Better than many. I see they're taking that one away, which means it's an hour past sunset, if there was a

118

sun to see. Better than corpse-carrying certainly, especially a corpse six days dead.'

'What happened to him?'

'What do you mean, what happened to him?' He turned from the window. 'Condemned to the Demons. What else?'

'Why? What did he do wrong?'

Johnson scratched his head. 'The General did say, but I don't rightly recollect.'

I asked further, and learned more. Condemnation to the Demons, unknown in the south, was a common occurrence here. Two weeks would be an unusual interval to pass without a sentencing, four unheard-of. And it was the General, not the Summoner, who did the condemning.

The matter-of-fact way in which Johnson detailed the procedure was almost worse than gloating would have been. The victim was condemned prior to the Summoning, and following the appearance of the Demons was roped to the Demons' Chair. After that the crowd dispersed to their homes and no one ventured out again, because during the night the Demons returned. This time they were seeking blood, and though a sacrifice had been prepared for them there was no certainty some other morsel of humanity might not prove tempting.

So doors were bolted, shutters tightly drawn. Those living close by would hear the howling of the Demons and, for a while, the screams of the victim. Not for long. In due course silence fell again, and the good citizens thanked the Dark One that they were spared, and went to bed.

I was both horrified and fascinated. 'What do the Demons *do* to them?'

'Shred their hearts within their living bodies,' Johnson said. 'You can tell by their faces next morning. Though no one looks close, not even the corpse-carriers. But their wrists are always bloody. That's from struggling to get free, when the Demons swoop.'

Market day provided a livelier view from my window. The square was thronged with carts and rows of stalls. The Demons' Chair stood empty, and people no longer avoided that area. A stall had been erected right beside it, from which sweetmeats were being sold. I heard the cry of the salesman – 'Toffee apples! Peppermint candy!' – and felt my stomach turn.

I thought of the life we had known in the Isles, and of our carefree wanderings with the gypsies, and wondered that this scene could be part of the same world. I wondered about Paddy too, and asked Johnson when he next appeared. He shrugged indifferently. She was being trained for a servant; as a southlander she'd have plenty to learn.

It would be unwise, I reckoned, to show too much curiosity, so I left it at that. Or to try to do things too quickly. The best plan was to gain Johnson's confidence over a period of days, at the same time gleaning as much as I could about the general situation. Neither my own confinement nor her being instructed in a servant's duties were great hardships. Eventually, if we caused no bother and kept our wits about us, there would be an opportunity for meeting and working out a way of escape. We had plenty of time for it.

Towards the end of the afternoon, market activity slackened, and the traders started packing up unsold wares and dismantling their stalls. Carts had entered the square that morning along several roads, and I expected a similar exodus; but though they formed up in lines they did not move off. Instead the tradesmen left them and made their way towards the gate leading to the General's house. They were joined by townspeople; soon there was a crowd converging on it.

As I was wondering about this, the door was flung open and Johnson stood there. In a brisker, more peremptory voice, he said:

'General's court. Everyone attends. Look sharp!'

He ignored my questions as he shepherded me downstairs and through a milling mass to a place at the front of the hall. The General's chair was empty, but there was a note of excitement and expectancy in the hum of voices. And there was the smell of a mob: unwashed and sour. Apprehension prickled the back of my neck. Why had I been brought here? Everyone attends, Johnson had said; but that might have been a way of making things easier for himself – he boasted of his skill in avoiding trouble. I moved, and his grip tightened on my arm.

There was a green door in the wall behind the dais, and the hum increased as it opened. Two guards appeared, followed by General Ramsay and a small boy similarly dressed in crimson; then two more guards. The guards took up posts on either side as he lowered his bulk into the chair; the boy put the stool in position and carefully raised the General's foot to rest on it.

The General's raised hand brought silence.

'Market day,' he said, 'and Demon's night to follow. That's the custom of our land and the will of the Dark One. It's also custom that a court be held to sentence evildoers.' He rubbed his cheek. 'Bring in Harold Openshaw.'

Two of the guards went out and returned, half-leading, half-dragging a small thin man, grey both in hair and face and sweating with fear.

'Harold Openshaw,' the blustering voice declared. 'Well known as a thief. Twice convicted, and now caught a third time, robbing from the Widow Galbraith. A month at hard labour for the first offence, two months for the second. What would you expect for the third but the Demons' Chair?'

Openshaw opened his mouth, but said nothing. His hand, his whole body, was trembling. The General touched his cheek again.

'Count yourself lucky, then, that tonight's culling has a riper candidate. Three months at hard labour.' He nodded to the guards. 'Take him out, and bring her in.'

She wore a shapeless black gown and her face was hidden by a veil. But this one was not dragged but walked defiantly between the guards, and I knew her walk as well as I knew those hidden features. I started to cry out, and Johnson's hand slapped hard across my mouth, stifling me.

General Ramsay said: 'A wench from the south – her name don't matter. She came into this decent law-abiding land wearing a yellow dress: showing her arms and legs, showing her face! Not content with that, she was impudent and insubordinate. She insulted her betters. She even dared lay hands on your General.'

With the boy's assistance, he stood up, and his face came into the light from the window opposite. When he dropped his hand, you could see the livid scratch-marks.

'Take her away,' the General said. 'Make her ready for the Chair.'

I tried to cry out again as Paddy was led off, but Johnson covered my mouth too closely. General and guards retired, and the crowd started to disperse.

'Have sense, lad. What good will bawling do?' Johnson relaxed his hold. 'That's better. I could tell you were a boy that's got his head screwed on.'

The hum of excitement continued round us. I saw gleaming eyes, ugly laughing faces.

'It's not easy when someone you know goes to the Chair. It's happened to me – one of the guards.' Johnson shook his head. 'I'd never much liked him, but the Demons' Chair . . . Yet it does no good to dwell on it. Look at it this way – by tomorrow it'll be over, and you'll still have your breakfast to eat. And she was a fool, your friend, when it comes down to it. The General's a queer one, but it's not too hard to find the way of doing what he wants. I mean, putting her nails into his face like that . . .'

He ushered me in front of him through the thinning crowd to the stairs. Where the stairs turned on themselves at the half-landing, I stooped down. Johnson said:

'What is it, lad? Something . . .?'

I did not rise but, taking a breath and tensing muscles, swung my body round and threw its full weight behind my flailing arm. As I hit him, Johnson lost balance and toppled backwards. I heard a single cry as I pelted down the stairs and out into the square.

9

One or two called out as I ran from the General's house, but only from indignation at being bumped into. There were no shouts from behind. I had heard Johnson fall heavily so he might have knocked himself out; but any confusion that did exist could not last long. If he were not in a condition to launch a pursuit, he had plenty of colleagues who would.

There was a muddle in the square, where traders were jockeying for position as they pulled out of line. They would need to get their goods home and unpacked, to be back in town for the Summoning. I dodged between them, at one point causing a horse to rear in the shafts and its owner to swear furiously at me. But that was commonplace anger at a carelessly running boy, and I was probably not the only one.

I had taken the road along which we had travelled the previous day, instinctively choosing a familiar route. I tried to visualize the way ahead: as I recalled, the densely-packed houses formed a kind of canyon, enclosing the road. I would be an easy target once a pursuit was launched.

I looked for a side street or alley but none was visible and I remembered thinking how far the dreary façade had stretched on our way in. When a gap did present itself it merely marked a drainage stream, guarded by a low stone parapet. The alarm must have been raised by now: I scrambled over the coping and slid down a slope. The base of the bridge was visible from the backs of the houses, but there was a culvert that offered concealment.

The stream was rain-swollen, but had been higher. I squatted in mud, head pressed against a slimy brick ceiling, and waited for my heart to stop pounding. Minutes after I had taken up my position, it pounded more heavily as hooves hammered the road above me.

I watched the narrow torrent flooding into the culvert. A twig was carried swiftly towards me, and as swiftly past to whatever destination chance might propose. I wondered if Paddy's fate, or my own, was any less random or inevitable. I had come a long way from the kitchen on Old Isle, and my childish conviction that there was no misfortune Mother Ryan could not put right.

My earlier complacency in thinking time was on our side mocked me. Although I, for the moment, was free, Paddy was a prisoner, facing an imminent and hideous death. Even if I knew just where she was being held, what hope was there of saving her? What chance did I stand against the General and his guards – still more against the Demons?

Mordecai had taught me that growing up meant learning things. Some things had to be accepted, but accepting defeat had not been part of his lessons. When I left, he had given me his gun. I remembered how he had instructed me in its use – saw again a flight of duck winging a twilit sky, his body turning in a matching arc, the double crack as he fired . . . and a feathered stone falling to earth. The image stirred something in my mind, at which I clutched desperately. Birds rode the sky. I felt a twitch of hope, and of excitement. And so did Demons!

I tried to estimate the distance to the spot where I had ditched the gun. It had taken about an hour to reach the camp, less than half that for the journey into town. It should be possible to manage the round trip in under four hours. The Summoning would be at dusk, but the Demons did not come back until some hours later. I had time to do it, if I wasted none.

Despite the best haste I could make, there were delays and setbacks. When I left the road to avoid the camp and its sentries, picking it up again was frustrated by tangles of brush that meant time-consuming back-tracking. The sky was rapidly darkening. In the dusk I sought landmarks, and several times imagined I was nearing my objective only to be disappointed. At one stage I took cover from what I thought was an approaching force: it proved to be a herd of wild goats, which stampeded when they scented me and bowled me over as they sped away. I thought I'd broken a leg, or badly sprained it, but the pain eased as I hobbled on.

I realized I had overshot my mark when the ruined cottage took shape in the gloom. Retracing my steps, I tried to work out how far we had gone before the second lot of horsemen surprised us. It wasn't easy. I came to the place where the brambles ended, and it occurred to me that I might not have thrust the gun far enough into them to deceive a keen eye. It might not be there any longer.

I plucked away swags which swung back stingingly, and peered into the tangle behind. If only there were a moon . . . but the clouds held it prisoner. As Paddy was.

How long had this quest lasted? It was full dark: the Summoning must be over. The square would be empty, citizens shut up in their houses, only Paddy left, bound, to await the Demons' return. Despondency overwhelmed me. Even if I *had* the gun, and got back with it before they came, what in fact could I do to save her? Demons might fly like birds, but that did not mean they could be struck out of the sky. Everyone knew they were creatures of the Moon: no earthly power could touch them.

With a numbed heart I contemplated the folly that had brought me here. There was nothing I could do to save Paddy, and I had been fooling myself in imagining it.

On the other hand, I was only a few hours from the crossroads where we had left the gypsies: I could catch up with them in a matter of days. Mordecai would ease the pain of thinking about Paddy. He would tell me I had done what I could, and help me bear the misery of failing her. I imagined telling him, and tried to imagine his response. But that scene would not come alive. Instead I heard his voice, on a windy day with sun and cloud chasing one another's tails and a smell of rain:

'Everything you do has to be thought through aforehand – careful and clear and honest.'

And now a question stabbed me like a dagger: what are you really doing here?

My reasoning had seemed straightforward: the gun would give me a chance to save Paddy from the Demons. But what had I overlooked? The answer came, sharp and bitter. Johnson had told me that people looked for places of safety once the victim was in the Chair. The square was left deserted. So if instead of this futile search I had found a hiding place in the town, I could have simply gone back and cut her free. And in fact I had found one: in the culvert.

'Careful and clear and honest' . . . I had been none of them, but especially not honest. Even a moment ago I had been looking to Mordecai to ease my conscience. That had been no better than self-pity, and despicable. But there was worse to contemplate. I had run away from the town, telling myself my aim was to return and rescue her. At the back of my mind, had I been thinking all along of heading for Mordecai, and safety? Had I been running from something I dared not face, though Paddy must?

There was blackness inside as well as out. I threw myself into the brambles, arms flailing, not sure if I was looking for the gun or for pain to ease the sharper anguish of remorse. But I scarcely felt the thorns that tore my skin – and then my hand touched something cold and hard.

I drew out the gun, and held it. It would not help, and nor could I. But there was only one road I could possibly take. I started running towards the town, with something worse than Demons at my back.

At one point the moon came out, and briefly rode a gulf between silvered clouds. Looking up as I ran, I wondered if the Demons were on the way from their cold white home, black wings flapping as they headed for their helpless victim. I almost thought I saw dots moving against the brightness, before the clouds closed up again.

I tripped and fell, stumbling on the unlit road, and later lost the road altogether and was obliged to trace a hard way back. I did not bother to make a detour of the camp and saw no sign of sentries; perhaps they too had hidden themselves. The town was silent when I reached it, empty apart from a prowling cat, only thin gleams of light showing behind closed shutters.

The square was quiet also. Approaching the tower I had a numbing fear that the Demons might have already come, and gone. I called Paddy's name, quietly and then louder. This time she answered weakly. I reached the Chair, and saw her hand try to move against her bonds.

Wasting no time in words I felt for the ropes, which were thick and tightly knotted. I found my knife, and sawed at the nearest strand. It was a slow business, and after it had parted she seemed no less securely held. In daylight I could have sought a key rope to sever, but in the dark could only tackle them as I found them. Paddy cried out once, when the blade slipped, but whispered:

'No – don't stop . . .'

It was a relief when the darkness began to lessen. I could see the strand I was working on more clearly. The moon, I thought, breaking through again. But the light became brighter, and brighter still; and looking up I saw it was not the moon.

An illumination was spreading out from the top of the tower. It looked beautiful and innocent, a silvery path of wonder; but with cowering heart I knew just what it was, and to what horror that radiance would give birth. Paddy knew too: I heard her moan.

It started as a single dot of jet in the centre of the brightness. The dot swelled, and budded, and opened like a flower; but the flower was a rotting face. Individual features showed clear – jagged bloody tooth, crumbling nose, baleful dripping eye – but the whole was a festering mess of corruption. I had seen it before, or something very like it, at Summonings. But here it was bigger, and closer, and the dripping eye was fixed on me.

Attached to the face was a body of equal foulness, sprouting boneless arms and clawed hands. I shrank away as the talons stabbed down at me, and the knife dropped from my nerveless fingers. Just when I was sure the claws must reach and rip me, the Demon swerved away. But a second had grown behind the first, and a third and fourth.

The howling had begun too, without words but full of hate and the promise of torment and death. It was many-voiced: the radiance had spawned more monsters than I could count and went on spawning more. They writhed in a snake-like tangle across the sky, weaving ghastly patterns from which individual fiends plunged down, each descent more terrifying than the last. Like cats with mice, it was a dance that must end in death. The patterns narrowed and converged towards the spot where I crouched in terror.

Brain and breast and bowels seemed on the point of bursting. I was gripped by an urge to run, though knowing I could not outrun them. Paddy moaned again, and I saw her in the stark light, bound and powerless.

It was not courage which stopped me fleeing, for I had none left. It was despair rather, and the bitter realization that I could not betray her a second time. As the next Demon swooped and its screeching drilled my ears, I fumbled for the gun. Blindly still, I found cartridges, broke open the breech, and pushed them into place. Somehow I got the gun to my shoulder, and fired.

For an instant the explosion blotted out all other sound; but from its echoes the howling rose again . . . and the faces were coming still, and the clawing hands. But how could it have been otherwise – how could anything fashioned by man even touch a creature from the moon? Mordecai had mocked at Demons, but Mordecai had not seen them as I saw them now.

Looking up at the chimney's top etched against the light, I recalled the words of his mockery. 'I've seed a sight of high places but never a Demon's nest . . . it's as though they're reserved special for sassenachs . . .'

They come out from tops of mills, he had said, or old chimney stacks, or tall masts. 'A Demon's nest . . .' Could it mean such places were their eyries, that it was there they lived and not in the distant Moon? It made no difference – if Demons were invulnerable, their nests must be too – but I still had a barrel loaded. Despair and hatred joined hands. Not blindly now but with cold purpose I lifted the gun, took aim on the chimney's top, and squeezed the trigger.

A second time the echoes of the explosion died; but this time into an aching silence. I looked at an empty sky, where the only light was from the moon, cruising a quiet sea between coasts of cloud. Sounds followed then, but no more than the clatter of falling fragments of brick and stone.

'What happened?' Paddy asked faintly.

'I don't know.'

'Cut me loose?'

I retrieved the knife and set to work. It wasn't long before the last strand parted, and I could help her out of the Demons' Chair.

We took the road that led most directly north. Our progress was not swift: Paddy was stiff and limped, from having been tied up. We did not speak. There could be ears behind the shutters of the houses we passed, tongues to wag next morning.

The town seemed to stretch even further in this direction, but at last we reached open country. The only signs of life were reclining cattle, breathing silvery plumes into the moonlight. When something ran across the road in front of us, Paddy asked 'What was that?' in curiosity rather than alarm.

'Charlie Fox,' I said, 'looking for breakfast.'

She said with feeling: 'I could do with some. The women said food would only be wasted on Demon fodder.'

I asked: 'Why *were* you condemned?'

'You were there.'

'But before that. You scratched Ramsay, didn't you? I saw the marks on his face.'

Paddy shook her head. 'I don't want to talk about it.'

It would be useless to persist, and I did not really want to. I told her about escaping from Johnson and going back for the gun. Knowing her gift for fastening on weak spots, I thought she might ask me why I'd thought that was a sensible idea, and didn't know what to say if she did. Though in fact, and in a way I still could not understand, the gun had saved us. But she picked on another point.

'You fired twice. The first shot didn't work.'

I explained that I'd aimed the second barrel not at the Demons, but their nest.

'I don't see why that should make a difference.' I had no answer. After a pause, she said: 'Do you think they'll come back – the Demons?'

'No. They've gone. They won't come back.'

I wished I were as confident as I hoped I sounded. The fact that I had shattered their nest and made them vanish meant they were less omnipotent than the landsmen believed. Had Mordecai and the Master been right about them all along? And yet despite what had happened, I could not credit it. With daylight there was certain to be pursuit and, if we were recaptured, another condemnation. I feared what would happen after that as much as ever. I wondered if they would rope us in the Chair together, or whether one of us would have to wait.

When moonlight faded into the new day, it showed a forest stretching as far as the eye could see. Not long after that, I noticed, to the west of the road, a pattern of lines within the tangle of green. While we were travelling with the gypsies we had encountered traces of the old times, before the Madness: mounds which had been houses, great masses where a town had stood. One area had stretched for several miles: it was hard to comprehend the number of people who must have lived there.

I had seen this pattern before too, and Mordecai had identified it as the relic of an orchard and pointed to fruits still growing, generations after the people who planted them had vanished.

'Over there,' I said. 'Apples?'

They were small, but red and crisp and sweet. We forced a way through the brush, and ate till we were full. Afterwards I flopped on a patch of grass for a rest, and was awakened by Paddy shaking me.

'I wasn't asleep,' I lied. 'And a minute or two will make no difference.'

'The sun's up.' She pointed. 'They'll have found the Chair empty by now.'

So we trudged on. Later we came on another vestige of the past in a shattered arch that must have been part of a bridge; and then a continuous succession of humps and ridges which told us we were crossing the ruins of a town. A tangle of creepers half-concealed a tilting pole, and while I was wondering what purpose it might have served, my eye picked up a dazzle of light ahead. Rain had brought about a slippage, exposing old stone. The reflection was from a window that still held glass, for the most part unbroken: small coloured panels forming a design. I remembered the ship in the window of the Master's house, and stopped to study it.

The window was in a building more than half buried: this would have been an upper section. Slabs of grey stone were shattered in places, but otherwise fitted close together. I found an opening: clearly the entrance to a badger sett but the slippage had enlarged it and created a tunnel wide enough to admit me.

As I edged in, Paddy protested: 'There's no time . . .'

I called back, hearing my voice echo: 'I just want to have a look. And if anyone did come, we'd be out of sight.'

Inside it was very dark, the only light filtered by the

coloured glass. I could see details more clearly from this side – there was a bearded face, an upraised hand, and a woolly lamb which strangely had a ribbon round its neck and a cross hanging from it. I supposed it must have meant something to our ancestors.

As my eyes became accustomed to the gloom, I made out stone pillars and panels of crumbling wood. There was a smell of badger, but no other sign: they would be deep inside their burrow at this time. A cloud crossed the sun outside, and the light dimmed.

When it brightened again, I noticed something else: a carved wooden figure, almost life-size, of a man, the lower part buried in rubble but the upper free. He had a post behind him, and his outstretched arms were fixed to cross-pieces. His chest was bare and there was a band of thorns round his head.

Paddy had followed me in.

'Who's that?' she whispered. I shook my head. 'Is he meant to be alive, or dead?'

'Dead.' I looked at the face which looked towards the light. 'No, alive.' I looked again. 'I'm not sure.'

'There's writing on the wall, up there.' It was in gold letters. Paddy read out haltingly: '"God so . . . loved the world . . ." I can't make out the rest.'

'What do you think it means?' I asked.

'I don't know. It's not what the Summoners say. But . . . if they were wrong . . . perhaps there need not be Demons?'

Towards the end of the morning the road became uphill, the gradient slight at first but rapidly turning steeper. We argued about resting: I was for getting off the road, Paddy for continuing. The further we got from the town, the less chance there was of being found. I said we had surely travelled far enough, but she shook her head and we plodded on.

As the road continued to climb, the woods thinned and finally gave way to heather-covered moorland. The sun was well down from its zenith, but it was hot still: we sweated, and dust from our scuffing feet painted us white. I pointed out that Paddy's hideous black dress – she said she would never again tolerate even a single black button – was black no longer, but she wasn't amused. I felt tired, but somehow light-hearted. She had been right to insist on pressing on. I had no idea where we would find shelter for the night, but we must be safe by now.

A pace or two ahead, I was aware of her stopping and looked back. She was looking back herself.

'It's them.'

Her voice was flat. Behind us the chalky ribbon of road led to the distant emerald stain of the forest; ahead it divided the emptiness of the moorland to an even more distant horizon. And, about a mile back, white dust rising against the blue sky signified horsemen: a dozen of them, maybe more.

'They may not have seen us,' I said. To the right there was nothing but heather, but to the left a few patches of brush. 'Come on!'

She shook her head, but went with my tugging hand. The first thicket was hopelessly thin, but one twenty metres beyond offered slightly better cover. Paddy had stopped though, looking back again, and I was forced to do the same. The riders had left the road and were heading across the moor in our direction.

They were only three or four hundred metres off, shouting at the gallop. Even if I managed to get the gun out and load it, there would be no point. And these had no nest to destroy.

The thin whine, rising and deepening, came from far

behind us. I wondered confusedly how a wind could get up so fast on a clear day. Nor could I understand what was happening to the horsemen: mounts were rearing, voices crying not in triumph but alarm. A couple of riders fell; others put up their arms, shielding their eyes.

I turned, and was forced to cover my own. A huge thing of fire, shapeless behind a coruscation of shimmering gold, was coming down on us. I remembered Andy: 'sweeping out of the sky in a fiery chariot . . .' The Demons had not waited for Ramsay's men to get us. They had come for us themselves.

Something detached from the golden glare, arcing across the sky to burst between us and the panic-stricken horsemen. While I looked they started to blur at the edges; as did heather and road, and the sky itself. My mind wavered with my vision, and I lost hold on both.

10

In my dream I was in the kitchen on Old Isle, shelling peas. I could not have been more than three or four years old because I was sitting on one of the ladder-back chairs, and had to reach a foot down to touch the floor. There was a smell of baking, and Mother Ryan was making pastry on the marble-topped table: gathering up dough, powdering it with flour and rolling it flat again. I was shelling peas from tightly-packed pods into a basin, scrupulously eating just one out of every pod.

And yet after all we were not in the kitchen but out of doors, with the sun warm on my bare arms and grass under my feet instead of tiles. Tiger, the bull terrier who died when I was four or five, scattered glistening droplets as he shook himself dry from the sea. I could hear Andy somewhere, singing a song about a soldier. But Mother Ryan was still rolling pastry, and I was still shelling peas.

When Mordecai came across the grass towards us I was not surprised; but I was embarrassed. He had the shotgun beneath his arm, and said something about going after pheasant. I knew there were no pheasants on the island, but, more important, going with him would mean abandoning the pea-shelling. I looked at Mother Ryan and she looked back, and I did not know what to do.

That was when the Demons swooped out of the sky, one menacing her and a second Mordecai. Somehow it was

I who now had the gun, but I could not make up my mind which Demon to fire at first. And Antonia was there as well – and Paddy. Other Demons were threatening them.

I woke with a pounding heart. It took me several moments to be sure there was no Mother Ryan here, no Mordecai . . . and no Demons. No sunlight either, or grass.

I tried to work out where I might be. There was a deep throbbing noise which seemed to come from all round. I was lying on a couch in a small chamber, of which one side was strangely curved, and there was a door in the facing wall. Paddy was asleep on a second couch. Diffuse illumination came from long panels in the walls: brighter than lamp-light, not so bright as daylight.

When I sat up, my foot encountered an unfamiliar resilient material, whose very strangeness convinced me this was no dream but reality. Reality *where*, though? I remembered the great noise in the sky and the fiery chariot. The Demons had come for us. Could we be on the moon?

I considered waking Paddy, but decided to find out more before I did. There were small windows in the curving wall and brighter light beyond. I went to the nearest, uneasily aware of the floor quivering beneath me. The window was no more than half a metre across, fitted with thick glass that reflected a distorted image as I drew near.

At first I was conscious only of sky more intensely blue than any I'd known, and a brilliant sun from which I had to avert my gaze. I looked down as well as out, and felt giddy. White smoke puffed and eddied beneath me. Was this the moon, or Hell? Would the smoke part to show the fires of the damned? I drew back; then stopped, and stared in fascination. The smoke formed shapes, and the shapes were of something I knew. I was looking at clouds – not from below, but above.

As I watched, the clouds divided, opening up a chasm. I

stared down a dizzying depth at a miniaturized landscape: pocket-handkerchief fields, the thin silver scrawl of a river, tiny houses and tinier cattle. The effect was magical, but deeply shocking. I realized I was trembling, and had to turn away. I was sitting on the edge of the couch, trying to make sense of it, when the door opened and a man came through.

'Your friend's still asleep?' He nodded towards Paddy. 'It's nothing to worry about. The effects vary. She probably inhaled more deeply.'

I could not place his accent, though it raised an echo. He was about forty, two metres tall, with a sombre face – high forehead, broad cheek-bones, deep-set deep grey eyes, thick black hair combed tightly back. His dress was a light-blue tunic over trousers ending at the knee. These were darker blue, and both garments were of a flimsy material that didn't seem like either cotton or silk. He had bare legs, and brown sandals which could have been leather but somehow looked different.

I didn't know what to say. He came to sit by me on the couch.

'It's bound to be a shock. Ask what questions come to mind, and I'll do my best to answer. Take your time.' He smiled, and his face was less forbidding. 'There's no hurry.'

'Where are we? I looked out . . .'

'That would be shock enough in itself, I imagine. Since you're up in the air, this ought to be a Demon's chariot. In fact, it's an aeroplane, which means nothing to you. A Z32 light aircraft, which means even less. Don't worry. Things will make sense, bit by bit.'

'The Demons . . .'

'That's easy. There are no Demons.'

'But I've *seen* them. Several times. I killed some. Or at least I destroyed their nest.'

He laughed. 'So you did, I gather! Or at any rate you smashed the transmitter, which amounts to the same thing. Perhaps I'd better try to give a general explanation and you can put the questions later. My name's Stephen, by the way.'

He offered a hand, which I took gingerly: the grip was reassuringly firm.

'I'm Ben.'

Stephen nodded. 'Yes, we know.'

Paddy stirred, and opened her eyes. Stephen let her wake before he told his tale.

It was a story that overturned everything I had taken for granted since childhood; but made sense of old doubts and uncertainties and also of many recent events. In the end there came a point at which the picture tilted, and my life as it had seemed till now became the upside-down one.

The world of our ancestors, he explained, had been full of marvels. After thousands of years of painfully slow advances a burst of discovery had come which seemed to have no limits. New forms of energy were developed, incredible machines invented. The picture in the book we had found was true – men had indeed travelled to the moon.

The population increased enormously, and came to live in bigger and bigger cities: eventually in super-cities comprising many millions. That was where things went wrong.

'Ants can live together like that,' Stephen said, 'but we're not ants. We belong to a species that functions best in small groups, where we're individuals relating to one another. We're a violent species too, and even in those groups we had to develop rules of behaviour to control our violence.'

I remembered, as he spoke, the little community in

which I had myself grown up, and my own minor angers and resentments. There had been rules there, laid down and administered by Mother Ryan with loving sternness.

'Those rules don't work where everyone's a stranger. Men and women had spent tens of thousands of years living in tribes, and suddenly there were no tribes any more. Parents lost control of themselves, and of their children. It was every man for himself, and woman too. Violence and murder became commonplace, eventually the normal way of life. They preyed on one another beneath the soaring towers of their cities. And when the horror of it became unbearable, they took drugs; which made them forget their misery for a time but in the end destroyed their minds. That was the Madness.'

'But what destroyed the cities?' Paddy asked.

'They weren't destroyed, simply abandoned when they became death-traps. People fled from them. And the machines stopped, with no one to tend them; and rusted away. Since everyone had come to depend on machines for food, millions died from starvation.'

I tried to think of millions. There had been seven of us on Old Isle, maybe two thousand in the whole of the Western Isles. A thousand times that number, dying of hunger surrounded by their great pitiless machines? I thought of the huge ship in the picture in the Master's house and wondered where it had last docked, to rust away with its crew of skeletons.

'Those who survived went back to simpler ways. They knew a terrible thing had happened, but couldn't understand why. They felt they were being punished, and that perhaps it was right they should be. They invented a punishing god, the Dark One, to give meaning to their lives. And they brought back strict codes of behaviour to make themselves feel safe, and launched little wars to justify the new tribes they were creating.'

'The new tribes,' I said, ' – those were the landsmen. What about the sea-people?'

'They were already separate,' Stephen said. 'At the height of the breakdown some had taken refuge in remote islands, hoping not only to escape but to preserve mankind's hard-won knowledge and use it to build a better civilization. As the chaos on the mainlands gave way to warring clans, they began to fear what might happen if the landsmen explored the seas again and threatened their peace.'

I said: 'The landsmen say it was the other way round – that they closed their ports to the sea-people for fear they might bring the Madness back.'

Stephen nodded. 'It suited us that they should think so. Just as it suited us for the landsmen to war with one another. Our people used the worship of the Dark One to help keep control. Originally, Demons were just a minor part of the religion of hell-fire and damnation. We had machines which could project images, and we sent expeditions to set them up in suitable places on the mainland.'

Suitable places ... That meant high up, where they couldn't be seen. I remembered Mordecai's comments about the Mill people and the Stack people, and the Mast people in the northern port. And I remembered the Demons' rules about buildings having to be not more than six times the height of a man. So that their nests, the locations where the projectors were installed, could not be overlooked.

I said: 'But didn't the landsmen see them doing it?'

'The aircraft were camouflaged with artificial flames, to look like Demons' chariots. And those areas were blanketed with a gas that produces temporary unconsciousness – the same one we used on you and those troopers. After the machines were put in, the Demons were programmed to appear at dusk on certain days.'

Paddy said: 'But the Demons come when the Summoners call them.'

Stephen said: 'It wasn't enough just to set up the machines. There had to be someone to interpret the wishes of the Demons. The Summoners do that.'

'You mean, Summoners are agents of the sea-people?'

I thought of Pengelly's Summoner, shrieking about hell-fire, and the dusk of Demons. Stephen said: 'It was a hard task, and a lonely one. And it meant a life of exile. But there were those who volunteered to do it.'

'Do the Demons have to be so frightening?' Even accepting that they weren't real, I shuddered at the memory.

'People don't choose a cruel god unless they want to be terrified. The more horrifying the Demons were, the more they flocked to worship them.'

Paddy said: 'Sacrificing men and women . . .'

'Was their own idea too. Not all tribes do it. The Stack people are more blood-thirsty than the rest.'

'How do they actually die,' she asked, '– the victims?'

'From fear. Long ago there were primitive people who would die when a witch-doctor pointed a bone at them. Demons are much more effective.'

'Yes.' Paddy's voice was low. 'I know.'

'It's a horrible business,' Stephen said, 'and I wouldn't attempt to justify it. But the way our people saw it at the time, they were simply trying to protect themselves. It was the landsmen who thought up the sacrifices.'

I said: 'But the killing Demons – the ones who frighten people to death – come twice, the second time when there's no one there but the person in the Chair.'

There was a silence before Stephen said: 'Some projectors were modified to provide a repeat performance. It was what the Stack people wanted.' Neither Paddy nor I spoke, and after a moment he went on: 'That was terribly wrong.

There were those who argued it was a lesser evil – that the landsmen's demon-worshipping religion gave them a kind of stability, and if it collapsed there would be chaos again on the mainlands, and much more misery and death. It wasn't a good argument. Our people made mistakes, and that was an unforgivable one. But mistakes can be corrected. Changes are taking place, big changes. That's why we were looking for you, Ben.'

I stared at him stupidly. 'For me?'

'Your father was the one known as the Master.' I nodded, though it wasn't a question. 'Before he went to the Western Isles he lived in Ireland, where he married your mother. And before that?'

'I don't know.'

But even as I spoke, I heard again a teasing familiarity in his accent and knew where I had heard it before. Stephen said:

'He was one of the sea-people. The tribes on the mainland are ruled by Generals, as you know. The islands have a governing council, with a leader known as the Custodian. Your father was Custodian.

'He saw the need for changes: for making an end not just to the Demons of the sacrifices, but all Demons. He wanted contact with the landsmen restored, so they could be educated out of their ignorance. He argued for it in the Council. Some agreed, but others were afraid an end to the Demons might mean an end their own good lives.

'They were in the majority. When your father wouldn't give in, he was offered the choice of death or exile. He accepted exile, in the hope that a future council might reverse that one's decision. But he didn't trust them. He took with him a device which would be activated when the surrounding temperature varied by more than a few degrees from normal blood temperature. When that happened, it would send a signal to a hidden transmitter and release a message calling on the sea-people to rise against the Council. He wore it next to his skin. It meant they were safe as long as he lived, but if he died his message would be released.'

'A round medallion,' I said. 'Silvery-grey metal, on a gold chain.'

Stephen nodded. 'It was a game of bluff. Your father's enemies wanted time to consolidate their position. He was a popular man but they hoped with the passing of time he would be forgotten, and the message would have no effect. But he wasn't forgotten. When he died and the message was broadcast, there was an uprising. That was when his enemies burnt his house in the Western Isles, in case it contained anything else that might damage them.

'Because the medallion was a transmitter, it could be traced. They discovered it had survived the fire and worked out you must have it: they knew you were his son. They thought they could make use of you, and sent a message through the Summoner of the Western Isles to hold you.'

'If Ben's father was so popular,' Paddy said, 'couldn't he have appealed to the sea-people at the time, instead of letting them banish him?'

'His enemies had a weapon of their own, in the shape of hostages. He had a wife before Ben's mother, and a son. He bargained for their safety. He thought his son might achieve what he hadn't been able to do.'

I felt a strange chill. A son he had acknowledged, and loved. 'Why did they need me, if they had him?' I asked.

'He died as a boy. There's only you left. And *we* need you now.'

'We?'

'The new Council. The revolution triumphed but there are still some who are opposed to change. You can help us, and I hope you'll want to. There are also entitlements. You inherit property in the islands, and certain rights. Above all, of course, the right to live as one of the sea-people.'

There was a pause before Paddy said, brightly: 'So you've come into your inheritance after all, Ben, even if it's not the one you expected.' She turned to Stephen. 'You may need him, but you won't need me.'

Before Stephen could speak, I said: 'I'm not going anywhere without her. You can keep the property and rights.'

He nodded. 'That's why we picked her up with you.'

'But *I* don't have to go,' Paddy said. 'Do I?'

I looked at her; she didn't look at me. Stephen said:

'I imagine you're thinking of your mother and sister. Ben can bring anyone he wants.'

I asked: 'Mordecai?'

'Who's that?'

When I explained, he said: 'So that's where you were when we lost touch. We found the medallion in a field near the villa. I suppose you dropped it.'

I shook my head. 'I threw it away.'

'It would have been a lot easier if you hadn't; and if you'd stayed at the villa till we were ready to get you. The next we knew, you were being held by Ramsay, and then that you'd escaped. It was a close-run thing, getting to you before his men did. As for the gypsy . . . you could bring him, but . . .'

There was no need to finish the sentence. This new life would hold no attraction for Mordecai. A traveller, he had said, following a known path. I looked at Paddy.

'You'll come, though?'

I didn't quite manage to keep the tremor from my voice. I needed her now more than ever.

She hesitated, but only briefly. 'Yes, I'll come.'

★

Much later, Stephen said: 'We're nearly there. Look.'

I followed him to the window. The sea below was sprinkled with ships and I could see the dots of people on their decks. There were other aircraft in the sky as well. It was a busy scene.

We were approaching a shore-line. Beyond it, fields and houses basked in sunshine. An inheritance after all, as Paddy had said. There would be all manner of new places to see, new things to do. And Paddy would be with me; in due course, Mother Ryan and Antonia too.

I thought of the Western Isles, which until a few months ago had been my world. A very small world, made up of hard work and simple living, with only a distant threat of Demons. Now the Demons were dead, and a bigger exciting world was opening up. I wondered if I could ever love it half as much.

THE LOTUS CAVES

Beneath the arid crust of the moon there grows an alien being – one both beautiful and terrifying!

When Marty and Steve break out of the moon Bubble, steal a crawler and go joyriding beyond the legal limits, they know they are in for trouble. But then the crawler crashes through the surface of the moon into an unknown and eerie world and they find themselves in more trouble than they had bargained for . . .

THE GUARDIANS

Accidents happen, they said – but was his father's death really an accident?

On the run after the tragic death of his father, Rob Randall risks capture, punishment and even worse when he crosses the Barrier into the open fields of the County. Life there is idyllic, almost feudal, and so long as Rob can hide his secret past, then he is safe. Or so he thinks . . .

A chilling story of life in the not-too-distant future, when power is held by a few and rebellion crushed mercilessly.